"You're suppose[d] ... [over the net.]

Elizabeth over the net.

"I *tried*," Elizabeth snapped back. "You could have gotten it if you had just moved a few inches."

Kimberly stomped her foot. "You have rotten aim!"

"Oh, yeah?" Elizabeth replied. "Well—you're lazy!"

"Come on, girls," Sandra called out. "Let's try it again."

"Do we have to?" Kimberly whined. "This isn't teaching us anything we don't already know."

"Stop complaining!" Elizabeth called to her.

Kimberly's eyes widened in shock. "Don't you dare tell me what to do!" she yelled back. "I'm the captain of this team. Not you!"

Elizabeth was so angry she could feel the blood pounding in her ears. Why did Kimberly insist on acting so stupid? Didn't she know they were on the same team?

"Why do you keep picking on me?" Elizabeth demanded.

"Because you ask for it!" Kimberly yelled.

"Girls!" Sandra came toward them. "Please—" Elizabeth frowned in confusion as, breaking off her sentence, Sandra gasped and slid to the ground. Her eyes rolled back in her head and then she went completely limp.

Hang out with the coolest kids around!

THE UNICORN CLUB

Created by Francine Pascal

Jessica and Elizabeth Wakefield are just two of
the terrific members of The Unicorn Club
you've met in *Sweet Valley Twins* books. Now
get to know some of their friends even better!

A sensational *Sweet Valley* series.

TEAM SWEET VALLEY

WIN ONE FOR SANDRA

Written by
Thomas John Carmen

Created by
FRANCINE PASCAL

BANTAM BOOKS
TORONTO • NEW YORK • LONDON • SYDNEY • AUCKLAND

WIN ONE FOR SANDRA
A BANTAM BOOK : 0 553 50504 1

Originally published in U.S.A. by Bantam Books

First publication in Great Britain

PRINTING HISTORY
Bantam edition published 1996

The trademarks "Sweet Valley", "Sweet Valley Twins"
and "Team Sweet Valley" are owned by Francine Pascal
and are used under license by Bantam Books and
Transworld Publishers Ltd.

Conceived by Francine Pascal

Produced by Daniel Weiss Associates, Inc,
33 West 17th Street, New York, NY 10011

Cover photo by Oliver Hunter

Bantam Books are published by Transworld Publishers Ltd,
61–63 Uxbridge Road, Ealing, London W5 5SA,
in Australia by Transworld Publishers (Australia) Pty Ltd,
15–25 Helles Avenue, Moorebank, NSW 2170,
and in New Zealand by Transworld Publishers (NZ) Ltd,
3 William Pickering Drive, Albany, Auckland.

Printed and bound in Great Britain by
Cox & Wyman Ltd, Reading, Berkshire.

To Robert Irwin Marks

ONE

"I feel great today!" Elizabeth Wakefield exclaimed.

Jessica, Elizabeth's twin sister, yawned broadly. "I feel like taking a nap."

The two girls were walking down Sweet Valley Beach. Elizabeth jogged in a little circle around Jessica, who wasn't moving very fast. "I feel like I could win the California Games all by myself!" Elizabeth added.

The California Games were the state championships for middle school students. They were held every other year. This year Elizabeth was on the Sweet Valley Middle School beach volleyball team— and she had a feeling that the team just might have what it took to make it all the way to the Games.

"By yourself?" Jessica raised her eyebrows. "Is this the same Elizabeth Wakefield who is always telling me there are no stars in volleyball?"

Elizabeth giggled. "You're right. Volleyball is a team sport. And that's one of the things I like best about it."

"Gymnastics is supposed to be a team sport too," Jessica said thoughtfully. "I mean, everyone's scores get added up to see which team wins the competition. But what I like about it is when I get to show everyone *I'm* the best one on the team."

Elizabeth laughed. "Somehow that doesn't surprise me."

Jessica and Elizabeth had such different personalities and interests that it was sometimes hard to believe they were identical twins. Physically, they were perfect copies of each other, right down to the tiny dimple in their left cheek. Both girls had long golden hair and sparking blue-green eyes, and they wore the same size clothes.

But that was where the similarities ended. Elizabeth was the more responsible, serious twin. A hardworking student, she loved to write and hoped someday to become a professional journalist. She was very proud of her position as editor of *The Sweet Valley Sixers,* the sixth-grade newspaper.

Jessica's interests were very different from her sister's. She was a member of the Unicorn Club, a group of girls who considered themselves the prettiest and most popular girls at Sweet Valley Middle School. Elizabeth loved her twin more than anyone else in the world, but she wasn't crazy about her friends. As far as she could tell, the Unicorns didn't care about anything besides clothes, parties, gossip, and boys.

Even the sports the twins were interested in reflected their personalities. Jessica loved gymnastics—partly because she got to spend lots of time in the spotlight. Elizabeth, on the other hand, was happy to share her victories with her five volleyball teammates.

The girls passed a group of boys, who looked old enough to be in high school. They had a portable radio and a cooler full of soda.

Jessica stopped in her tracks, her eyes dancing. "This looks like the perfect spot for a rest!" She spread her towel a few feet from the boys.

Elizabeth giggled. She knew that Jessica's spending a quiet afternoon at the beach was about as likely as finding a snowball in the Sahara Desert. Especially since Jessica's best friend, Lila Fowler, was supposed to meet her any minute. "Well, I'd better go to practice," Elizabeth said. "Don't get too tired resting up!"

"Remember to keep your arm straight!" Sandra Kimbali, Elizabeth's volleyball coach, called out later that afternoon. The team was in the middle of a serving drill.

Elizabeth tossed the ball into the air with her left hand and hit it with her right fist. The ball flew over the net hard and fast.

"Nice one!" Sandra called out from the sidelines.

Ellen Riteman, who was on the other side of the net, neatly stopped the ball. She tossed it under the net to Maria Slater, who was behind Elizabeth in line.

Elizabeth grinned as she ran back to the end of the line. Sandra had a way of making Elizabeth feel great about her game—and herself. Elizabeth thought Sandra was the perfect coach: enthusiastic, energetic, and encouraging. Maybe that was why she had won so many coaching awards.

Sandra didn't usually coach middle school kids. Normally, she coached the women's volleyball team at Sweet Valley University. She had led the university's women's volleyball squad to three straight collegiate championships. But now that she was on maternity leave from the university, Sweet Valley Middle School hired her for a short time to coach its own volleyball team.

"Go, Maria!" Elizabeth called.

Maria served. The ball flew out of bounds. Sandra jumped nimbly to the side just before it hit her.

Maria cringed. "Sorry!"

Sandra leaned over to pick up the ball. "That's OK!" she told Maria. "You'll get it next time."

As far as Elizabeth could tell, Sandra hadn't let the fact that she was seven months pregnant slow her down at all. She had a funny habit of rubbing her rounded stomach, but otherwise, it was easy to forget she was pregnant.

Sandra had been coaching Team Sweet Valley for only two weeks. But Elizabeth could already see how much better they were playing. With Sandra's help, Team Sweet Valley had a good chance of taking first place in the California Games.

But first they had to make it *into* the Games. If they could do it, they'd be the first volleyball team from Sweet Valley to ever compete in the Games. The final qualifying match was just two weeks away.

Before then, the team would play matches against four other area middle schools. The two teams with the most wins in those matches would move on to the qualifier. Sweet Valley's first match was on Tuesday—four days away. Elizabeth figured that was why practice that afternoon was a little more intense than other practices had been. She was taking the drills and scrimmages more seriously than ever before. And she knew her teammates were working hard too.

Sandra tossed the ball to Kimberly Haver, who was next in line. Maria came to stand behind Elizabeth. "Having fun?" she asked.

Elizabeth wiped her sleeve across her forehead and grinned at her friend. "Definitely! Sandra's great."

"Yeah, she's pretty awesome," Maria said. "I wish I could say the same thing for my serve!"

Elizabeth didn't like to admit it, but Maria was right: Her serve could be stronger. But Maria was a great defensive player. She could block just about any ball that came whizzing over the net.

"You're up," Maria told Elizabeth.

Elizabeth stepped into place and carefully served again. The ball sailed over the net.

Maria's next serve also went over.

"Looking good," Sandra called.

Back in line, Elizabeth watched Cammi Adams get ready to serve.

"I'm really glad I made the team," Elizabeth told Maria.

Maria's eyes were sparkling. "And I'm glad I talked you into trying out."

A few weeks earlier, Maria had dragged Elizabeth to the court to try out for the team. Even though Elizabeth loved playing volleyball in gym and with friends on the beach, she hadn't really thought she was good enough to play competitively. But in the few weeks since she had made the team, Elizabeth's volleyball game had gotten powerful. Surprisingly powerful. Of course, playing on a real team with a coach and the best players at Sweet Valley Middle School was very different than just hitting the ball around with friends. It was more exciting. And the fact that Maria, one of her best friends, was on the team made it even more special.

Cammi served. But the ball hardly made it over the net.

"Give it a little more power next time!" Sandra called.

"OK," Cammi called back sheepishly.

Elizabeth liked Cammi a lot. She was one of the *Sixers* star writers and a really nice person. But Elizabeth secretly considered her the weakest member of the volleyball team. She did have one advantage over the other girls, though. Inches. Cammi had shot up over the past few months. She was a whole head taller than Elizabeth now. She was a great blocker, but her jumping was still too awkward.

Kimberly looked confident as she stepped into the service area. She was a seventh grader, the oldest girl on the team. She was also team captain.

"Get ready!" Kimberly called to Ellen. "This is going to be a killer serve."

Ellen giggled. "I'm ready!"

"I just hope she doesn't get that outfit dirty," Maria whispered to Elizabeth.

Elizabeth smiled and shook her head. Kimberly was wearing an expensive-looking shorts and T-shirt set. She'd tied a purple ribbon in her thick black braid. Like the other members of the Unicorn Club, Kimberly was *very* into fashion. But Elizbeth knew that she took her game seriously. In fact, Kimberly was one of the team's offensive stars. She could spike the ball over the net so hard it was almost impossible to block. And she would never hold back to keep her clothes clean—or for any other reason.

Kimberly's serve sailed over the net.

Ellen had to dash after it.

"Beautiful!" Mandy Miller called to Kimberly. On her way back in line, Kimberly slapped a high five with Mandy.

Mandy ran into the service area. She got the ball from Ellen and gave it a good whack. But the ball didn't leave her hand.

"Weird," Mandy muttered, looking puzzled. She drew her arm way, way back and hit the ball with all of her might. It still didn't budge.

"What's the problem, Mandy?" Sandra called.

"I don't know," Mandy said. "The ball's stuck. Hey—you don't think this could have anything to do with the cotton candy I just ate, do you?"

Maria groaned.

Elizabeth laughed. Mandy was one of the biggest clowns in Sweet Valley Middle School. Elizabeth sometimes had a hard time believing Mandy was a

Unicorn. She was much less snobby than the other members of the club.

Sandra walked onto the court and put her arm around Mandy's shoulders. "I think this little joke is Mandy's way of saying she's bored with the drill."

"Well, maybe a *bit*," Mandy said, making a goofy face.

"Fine," Sandra said. "Let's move on to a scrimmage. Mandy against everyone else."

Mandy's jaw dropped. She looked horrified.

"Got ya!" Sandra said with a wink. "Elizabeth, Cammi, why don't you give Mandy a little help?"

Elizabeth smiled to herself as she jogged into place. A coach who could out-kid Mandy Miller. How could you get cooler than that?

"All right, I'm going to set up some digs for you!" Sandra called out. A dig is a special kind of offensive move where the player dives to save the ball just before it hits the sand.

Elizabeth was soaked in sweat from the scrimmage. Her legs felt like they were made of lead. But when her turn came, she eagerly ran out onto the court. She threw herself on the sand, scooping up the ball and sending it flying up just seconds before it hit the ground.

"That was amazing!" Cammi told Elizabeth.

"Thanks," Elizabeth said, a little out of breath. She was always psyched when her moves were totally on target.

"That's it for today!" Sandra announced. "Great practice! So great, I'd like to take you all out for ice cream."

"Ice cream?" Ellen repeated. "Aren't we supposed to be in training?"

Sandra grinned at her. "You need to keep up your strength, don't you? And besides, I'm dying for a banana split!"

TWO

"I'd like a banana split with vanilla ice cream," Sandra told the waiter at Casey's. "Easy on the hot fudge. No, wait—make that two."

"Two banana splits," the waiter repeated as he scribbled on his order pad.

"And don't forget the whipped cream and nuts," Sandra added.

"How could I forget?" the waiter smiled wryly. "It's your usual."

"True!" Sandra's chocolate-brown eyes were sparkling.

Elizabeth raised her eyebrows as the waiter walked away. "You order *two* banana splits often?"

Sandra shrugged. "Ever since I got pregnant I crave ice cream. My doctor says it's OK if I indulge once a week. And today is the day!"

"You really know how to indulge!" Kimberly said.

Sandra winked at her. "Well, don't tell my doctor. He doesn't know how *much* ice cream I'm eating on my big indulgence day. I think a single scoop is what he had in mind."

"Don't worry. We won't tell," Cammi told Sandra.

"Yeah. It'll be kind of a team secret," Mandy added.

Elizabeth looked around at her teammates with satisfaction. Everyone had crowded around one big round table. And everyone was getting along great, which was amazing. At school, the team members would never hang out together. The Unicorns would stick with other Unicorns. Cammi, Maria, and Elizabeth would be with their friends. But Sandra made them forget about all that. Her enthusiasm for the team was contagious.

"Here you are!" the waiter said, setting their orders in front of them.

As Elizabeth took the first bite of her mango ice cream, Sandra gave her a big grin. "I'd never even *heard* of mangos when I was your age. Mango ice cream would be considered pretty exotic stuff in Kansas."

Elizabeth raised her eyebrows. "You're from Kansas?"

Sandra nodded. "Born and bred."

Elizabeth realized she didn't know much about Sandra. "When did you start coaching?" she asked her.

"About five years ago," Sandra told her. "My game was shot, so it was time."

"I doubt that!" Maria stated.

"No, it's true," Sandra insisted. "I was slowing down. As a matter of fact, I was never a really *great* player. I didn't have much natural talent."

"How can you say that?" Kimberly asked. "You were a terrific player! You were even on the Olympic team."

Elizabeth's eyes widened. "You went to the Olympics?"

"I sure did." Sandra turned to Kimberly. "How did you know?"

"My dad is a total volleyball freak," Kimberly explained. "He recognized your name immediately."

Maria grinned broadly at Sandra. "You must have been an incredible player."

Sandra shook her head. "I got to the Olympics on pure will," she said. "I loved the game so much that I worked really hard. And I managed to surpass some girls who were actually better players than I was. 'Work hard' was my motto." Sandra took a bite of her banana split, smiling at Elizabeth.

Elizabeth sat up a little straighter in her chair. Sandra was singling her out as an example of someone who worked hard!

Elizabeth glanced down at her empty dish, feeling embarrassed. "Yeah, I guess I have been working hard," she said modestly. "Of course, it's worth it considering how much I love—"

"Thanks for noticing." Mandy's voice rose over Elizabeth's.

Noticing what? Elizabeth wondered. She glanced up and saw that Sandra was smiling at Mandy.

I was wrong, Elizabeth realized, horrified. Sandra had meant Mandy was hardworking. Elizabeth's face was hot enough to burst into flames. She'd just made a complete fool of herself in front of all of her teammates—and Sandra.

Elizabeth decided this was a good time to change the subject. "Anyway, so, um, what were the Olympics like?" she asked, trying to cover up her embarrassment.

"The Olympics were great," Sandra replied. "And it was an honor to be there. But do you know what I really remember from my days as a player?"

Elizabeth shook her head.

"My happiest memory is winning the California Games when I was in middle school," Sandra told them. "That's one reason I jumped at the chance to coach Team Sweet Valley."

Kimberly wrinkled her nose. "How could the California Games have been so special? I mean, compared with the Olympics?"

Sandra laughed. "Well, it may be hard for you to believe, but the California Games were actually more exciting."

"No way!" Ellen said.

Sandra laughed lightly. "It's true. I played well in the Olympics. So did everyone on my team. But that's what everyone expected. In the Olympics, excellence is the standard. But my team was the underdog in the California Games." Sandra smiled at the memory. "When we started to win—and kept on winning—we became heroes at our school. My teammates and I became wildly popular."

Ellen's eyes lit up with interest. "Popular?" she repeated.

"Wildly," Sandra said with a wink. "It was fun."

Kimberly nodded knowingly. "That *is* fun."

"Definitely," Ellen agreed.

Maria and Elizabeth exchanged amused glances. Elizabeth had to force herself to keep a straight face. Kimberly and Ellen obviously considered themselves wildly popular.

"Did you get asked out on a lot of dates?" Mandy asked enviously.

Sandra's eyes were dancing. "So many I lost count."

"Did you go out with a lot of different boys?" Kimberly asked, leaning closer to Sandra.

"No, I concentrated on just one," Sandra said with a wicked grin. "The *cutest* one."

Mandy giggled. "What did he look like?"

"Wavy brown hair, huge dark eyes—your basic dream boat," Sandra replied.

"And is he the man you married?" Ellen whispered, leaning forward.

Sandra burst out laughing. "Oh—that would have been romantic! But I met my husband, Hank, in college. The dream boat moved to Alaska when we were in the eighth grade. But we had a great year. When I made time for him, that is."

"I thought you said he was your only boyfriend," Kimberly said.

"He was," Sandra replied. "But I had other interests too. During the games, I wrote a series of articles for the school paper. I won a student journalism prize for it."

"Wow!" Elizabeth exclaimed. "Those prizes are really competitive." She had heard a lot about the awards and she dreamed of winning one herself someday.

Sandra nodded. "I was thrilled to get it! I framed

the certificate they gave me. I still have it hanging in my study. If I hadn't become a coach, I definitely would have been a journalist."

"That's so cool," Maria whispered to Elizabeth.

Elizabeth nodded. Sandra seemed more impressive than ever. Not only was she a super volleyball player who'd worked hard enough to make it to the Olympics, but she'd been a prize-winning journalist too.

Sandra looked down at her empty dishes. "Are you kids almost ready to go? Hank probably has dinner almost ready by now."

"I'm ready," Mandy said.

Everyone started to get up.

The waiter came up with the check. "Was everything OK?" he asked.

"Great," Sandra told him. "But could I get a pint of vanilla to go?"

"Sure," the waiter said.

"You're going to eat more ice cream?" Ellen asked incredulously.

"For dessert," Sandra replied. "My indulgence day isn't over yet!"

"Where's Jessica tonight?" Janet Howell, president of the Unicorn Club, demanded later that evening. Most of the Unicorns had gathered at Kimberly's for a slumber party.

Kimberly was sitting on the floor, brushing Mandy's hair. She never would have admitted it, but Janet made her a tiny bit nervous. Janet could use her position to make Kimberly's life miserable if she wanted. Staying on her good side was all-important.

"Jessica is going on a trip with her family tomorrow morning," Kimberly replied. "They're leaving at six in the morning or something crazy like that."

Janet shuddered, then focused on her toenails, which she was painting purple, the official Unicorn color.

"How do you want me to do your hair?" Kimberly asked Mandy.

"I want to look glamorous," Mandy said thoughtfully. "Can you make my hair look like Sandra's?"

"You wish!" Ellen said, looking up from the magazine she was reading.

"What does Sandra's hair look like?" Lila Fowler asked, helping herself to a handful of popcorn.

"Blond and super curly," Mandy told her. "It's beautiful."

Lila made a face. "You just think it's beautiful because you worship Sandra."

Kimberly felt a flash of irritation. "We don't *worship* her."

Grace Oliver giggled. "Sorry, Kimberly, but Lila has a point. You guys talk about Sandra constantly. And you make her sound like she's a rock star or something."

"We do not!" Ellen exclaimed.

"Do too!" Grace insisted.

"I'm glad Kimberly and Mandy like their coach," Janet said in a queenly voice. "She's helping them get to the California Games. And that's going to look good for all of the Unicorns." Janet turned to Kimberly. "Make sure you mention the Unicorn Club to the reporters who interview you after you win. And if they want to talk to me, that's no problem."

Kimberly felt a stab of worry. Janet got very excited whenever the Unicorns won anything—probably because she thought all Unicorn successes reflected on *her* success as president. And now Janet seemed to think the volleyball team was definitely going to the Games. But as much as Kimberly wanted to go to the Games too, she knew it was a long shot. Somehow she had to remind Janet of that without sounding like a quitter. Janet hated quitters.

"So how are things going on the team?" Grace asked. "I mean, besides the fact that your coach is the greatest thing since low-fat pizza."

"Great!" Mandy said.

"OK . . ." Kimberly replied at the same time. *I have to make sure Janet blames someone else if we lose,* she decided. *Why not Miss Priss, Elizabeth Wakefield?*

Elizabeth was Kimberly's least favorite person on the volleyball team. She was always acting as if she were Sandra's little pet—maybe because all of the teachers at school were constantly drooling over her, telling her what a great student she was. Well, things on the volleyball team were going to be different. Kimberly was determined to be the star *and* Sandra's favorite player. For once, Elizabeth was going to have to step out of the spotlight.

Mandy turned around and looked at Kimberly. "Why just OK?"

Kimberly heaved a great sigh. "I just wish all of our teammates were Unicorns," she said.

The other girls nodded sympathetically.

"I don't know where Cammi Adams shops, but her clothes are a disaster," Kimberly went on. "And Jessica's sister bugs me," she added as casually as she could.

"I know what you mean about Elizabeth," Janet said, instantly taking Kimberly's bait. "She's just so— nice. And I agree it would be better if the entire team were Unicorns . . ."

Janet broke off and her face grew thoughtful. Kimberly bit back a smile. Janet was obviously impressed by her Unicorn spirit.

Then Janet pointed a finger at Kimberly. "But the fact that not all of us are on the team is all the more reason for you guys to win for the rest of us. You're team captain, Kimberly," she said forcefully. "The Unicorns are counting on you. Make sure the volleyball team wins."

"No problem," Kimberly told Janet with her most confident smile. But her stomach was doing flip-flops. *There's no way around it,* Kimberly thought with dread. *Janet will blame me if the volleyball team loses. And that means we have to win. No matter what.*

"Not so hard," Mandy cried out as Kimberly yanked the brush through her hair.

"Sorry," Kimberly muttered.

As soon as Kimberly stopped pulling so hard, Mandy relaxed. Her friends started to discuss their latest crushes, but Mandy was still thinking about volleyball. She loved playing on the team. As much as she liked clowning around, she was excited that she had found something that demanded serious concentration.

Thanks to Sandra, Mandy was discovering just how focused she could be. Sure, she had other interests—theater and fashion, for instance. She was an expert at putting together funky outfits from clothes she found at thrift shops. But somehow volleyball was different. Now she had a specific goal to reach. And a specific person to prove herself to: Sandra. *Janet shouldn't worry,* Mandy thought. *I'm going to make sure we make the California Games. Not so Janet can get her picture in the paper, but to make Sandra proud. And to prove to myself that I can do it.*

"Which sweater do you think I should pack?" Jessica asked, bounding into Elizabeth's room that night at ten o'clock. "Pink or purple?" She held two sweaters up in front of her.

Elizabeth put down the book she was reading in bed and stretched beneath the covers. "Pink."

Jessica gave Elizabeth a suspicious look. "Are you just saying that because you don't want me to look like a Unicorn all weekend?"

Elizabeth grinned. "You have to admit, it would be a nice change. And Aunt Helen doesn't care what you wear."

"I guess that's true," Jessica said, plopping down on Elizabeth's bed. "So are you all ready to go?"

The entire Wakefield family was going to spend the rest of the weekend at the twins' Great-Aunt Helen's house, which was a few hours away.

Elizabeth was psyched to see Great-Aunt Helen, one of her favorite relatives.

"Actually I haven't packed yet," Elizabeth said.

Jessica slapped her forehead dramatically. "What? You mean, I've actually packed before my superorganized sister?"

Elizabeth giggled as she fell back against her pillows. "I'm too tired to pack tonight. I'll do it in the morning."

Jessica put her hands on her hips. "Well, I hope you know what you're doing. I stayed home from Kimberly's slumber party so we could leave early tomorrow. I don't want to spend all morning waiting for you."

Elizabeth rolled her eyes. "Yeah, right. When has *that* ever happened?"

Jessica's eyes twinkled. "I guess not that often." She stood up and turned to leave. "But make sure you don't oversleep!"

As soon as Jessica was gone, Elizabeth flicked off the light. Her muscles ached—even though she had spent an hour soaking them in a hot tub. Still, Elizabeth was happy. The volleyball team was wonderful. And they had the most wonderful coach in the whole world.

As Elizabeth settled deeper into the covers, she decided she wanted to do something nice for Sandra. The perfect idea popped into her mind almost immediately. She could have a baby shower for her! The other girls on the team could help her plan it.

Elizabeth remembered how embarrassed she felt

when she had mistakenly thought Sandra was singling her out. Well, just because Sandra hadn't singled her out that day, it didn't mean she never would. Elizabeth knew she was the hardest worker on the team. Now all she had to do was convince Sandra.

THREE

"Hi, Maria!" Elizabeth said on Monday morning. She hurried over to where her friend was standing by her locker.

Maria looked up and grinned at Elizabeth. "Hi! How was your trip?"

"Pretty fun, but Jessica thought I was a total bore," Elizabeth admitted. "I kept nodding off. On Saturday night, I practically fell asleep at the dinner table."

Maria laughed as she closed her locker. "Me too! Mom made me go to bed at about eight o'clock. And I didn't even mind. Sandra worked us so hard last week, I felt like a zombie the whole weekend."

Elizabeth snapped her fingers. "Speaking of Sandra, I had a great idea over the weekend," she said as they started to walk down the hall. "I want to plan a baby shower for her. Mom already said it was OK to have it at our house."

"Actually, it's too late," Maria said.

"What do you mean?" Elizabeth asked. "Sandra isn't going to have her baby for almost six weeks."

Maria laughed and shook her head. "What I meant is that Mandy is *already* planning a shower. She called me about it yesterday."

Elizabeth frowned. "Why didn't Mandy call me?"

Maria shrugged. "You were out of town. She probably planned to tell you this morning."

Elizabeth sighed. She couldn't help feeling like Mandy had stolen her idea. But Elizabeth knew she wasn't being fair. Mandy and she had probably had the idea at about the same time. But Elizabeth had gone away that weekend—that was what let Mandy get ahead of her. "Well, I guess there's no point in both of us planning a shower," Elizabeth said reluctantly.

"One is probably enough," Maria agreed with a smile. "Mandy's going to invite the whole team, of course. And she even mentioned going in together on a present so that we can get something really nice for Sandra."

"I was going to suggest that too," Elizabeth said, trying to keep the disappointment out of her voice.

But Maria looked at her with concern. "Is something wrong?"

Elizabeth forced a smile. "I was looking forward to planning the shower myself," she admitted. "But I'm sure Mandy will do a great job."

Maria nodded. "If there's one thing Unicorns are good at, it's planning parties."

"Is everyone ready to get to work?" Sandra called out that afternoon as she walked toward the court. Her hair was pulled back in a high ponytail, and she was wearing a baggy red T-shirt.

"I am," Elizabeth said enthusiastically.

Kimberly shot Elizabeth a mean look. "Me too!"

"Great," Sandra said. "OK, team, let's get warmed up."

As the players spread out on the sand to stretch out, Elizabeth noticed there was less joking and laughing than usual. Even Mandy looked serious. *I guess everyone is thinking about our big match tomorrow,* Elizabeth thought.

While she was doing her toe-touches, Elizabeth caught Kimberly's eye and smiled at her. Kimberly quickly glanced away.

What's wrong with her? Elizabeth wondered. Then she shrugged. Kimberly may have been a great volleyball player, but she sure wasn't the friendliest person on earth. In fact, she could be incredibly irritable and bossy. Elizabeth just had to concentrate on her game.

"OK," Sandra said after the girls were warmed up. "Our first match is tomorrow. Rather than work on drills, I want us to spend most of today playing a three-on-three scrimmage. I'll be watching to see how your game is holding up. Kimberly, you and Elizabeth and Mandy on one side."

Elizabeth's heartbeat quickened with excitement.

During the matches that were coming up, all six girls would play together at the same time. Scrimmages, with just three girls on each side, were twice as strenuous.

Kimberly picked up the ball. "I'll serve first," she told Elizabeth and Mandy.

"Fine," Mandy said.

Elizabeth sighed. Kimberly was being her bossy self. But Elizabeth took a position close to the net without saying anything.

Kimberly served. The ball whizzed by Cammi before she had time to react.

"Beautiful!" Sandra called out from the sidelines.

Kimberly gave Elizabeth a triumphant look.

Elizabeth smiled back at her, feeling a bit uneasy. Why was Kimberly acting so competitive? Last time she'd checked, they were both on the same team.

Maria threw the ball under the net. "That's OK," she called to Cammi. "We'll get them next time."

"We'd *better*," Ellen put in.

Kimberly served again. Another ace. This time Cammi and Maria both tried to block it. Both missed.

"Way to go!" Elizabeth held out her hand so Kimberly could slap her a high five.

But Kimberly was eagerly looking off toward Sandra. "Hey, coach, how did that look?" she called.

Sandra laughed lightly. "Looked like an ace. Keep it up."

Kimberly served again. This time Ellen blocked

the ball. Cammi set it up perfectly and Maria hammered it over to Elizabeth's side of the court.

Mandy blocked the ball neatly. Kimberly set the ball up for Elizabeth to spike over the net. Elizabeth jumped up and hit the ball toward Cammi as hard as she could.

Cammi didn't even come close to blocking it.

"Would you wake up?" Ellen snapped at Cammi.

"Sorry," Cammi mumbled.

Maria gave Cammi a halfhearted pat on the back.

Elizabeth felt bad for Cammi, but she couldn't help being proud for scoring a point. As long as she kept that up, Sandra would have to notice how hard she played.

Kimberly's next serve went into the net. She frowned as she passed the ball under the net to the other team.

"Good job!" Elizabeth called to her. After all, most of Kimberly's serves had been perfect.

Kimberly glared at her. "You don't have to rub it in," she spat out.

Elizabeth caught her breath. "Rub it—?" Suddenly, she realized that Kimberly thought she was being sarcastic. "I wasn't rubbing it in! I was talking about, you know, your turn in general," she stammered. "I thought you did a really good job."

"Thanks," Kimberly said snidely. "But I don't need *you* to tell me I did a good job. I already know that."

Elizabeth glanced at Mandy. "What's wrong with her?" she whispered.

Mandy shrugged. "Let's get ready for the serve!" she said.

Ellen served the ball.

Elizabeth blocked Ellen's serve easily and passed the ball back to Kimberly.

"Mine!" Kimberly called. But instead of passing the ball forward to Mandy who was in position to spike, she bunked it over the net as hard as she could.

Elizabeth and Mandy both turned to stare at Kimberly.

The players on the other side seemed surprised too. Cammi let the ball hit the sand without touching it and Ellen didn't even yell at her.

"What are you doing?" Mandy demanded. "I was wide open."

"I'm just playing hard like Sandra told us to," Kimberly said with a shrug. "And it worked. We scored."

Kimberly sure is acting weird, Elizabeth thought. *She's always played aggressively—but this is ridiculous.*

"Look lively out there!" Sandra called from the sidelines. "Come on, Elizabeth, it's your turn to serve. Let's see if you can do as well as Kimberly."

Kimberly tossed her hair over her shoulder and beamed at Sandra.

As Elizabeth stepped into position, she felt a flash of jealousy. She suddenly realized what Kimberly was up to. She was trying to impress Sandra. The exact same thing Elizabeth was trying to do. The only difference was that Kimberly was probably succeeding.

Well, two can play at that game, Elizabeth told herself. *I'm going to play even harder for the rest of practice. We'll just see who impresses Sandra.*

"Great practice!" Sandra said after she blew her whistle to signal the end of the scrimmage. "Thanks, girls."

Elizabeth flopped down on the sand, exhausted. Her shorts and T-shirt were soaked in sweat. But she was positive she had impressed Sandra. In fact, she could hardly wait to hear all the nice things Sandra would say about her.

"Now I want you all to go home and get some rest," Sandra said. "Tomorrow's a big day—our first match!"

Elizabeth glanced up. Sandra was picking up her stuff and getting ready to go. *That's all?* Elizabeth thought sourly. Why hadn't Sandra said anything nice about her? Was it possible that she *still* wasn't working hard enough?

Maria got to her feet and held a hand out toward Elizabeth. "Ready to head home?"

Elizabeth tried to forget her disappointment. "Not really," she said, glancing at Sandra. "It's still early. I'm not tired—are you?"

Maria followed Elizabeth's gaze. "Tired? Oh, no, not at all. Why don't we stay and practice our volleys? Just for a little while, I mean."

Elizabeth grabbed Maria's hand and jumped to her feet. "That's a great idea!" Somehow, she imagined that when Sandra was training for the California Games, she practiced overtime.

Maria got her practice ball out of her gym bag. She and Elizabeth started to hit it back and forth over the net.

"What are you guys doing?" Cammi called. She was starting out of the parking lot on her bike.

Elizabeth stopped the ball and tucked it under her arm. "We're just getting a little extra practice in," she told Cammi. "Want to join us?"

Cammi glanced at her watch. "Well, I need to get home soon."

"Come on!" Maria said. "It'll be fun. And we're not going to stay for long."

"Well, OK," Cammi agreed finally. "I guess I could hang around for a few more minutes."

Cammi walked onto the court on Maria's side. But before the girls could start to play, Mandy ran up. "You guys want even teams?" she called.

"Sure!" Elizabeth called back.

The foursome started to hit the ball back and forth over the net. While they were playing, Kimberly and Ellen came up.

"What are you guys doing?" Kimberly demanded. "If you're holding an extra practice, why didn't you invite us? I *am* the team captain, you know."

Maria rolled her eyes. "Calm down," she told Kimberly. "We weren't leaving you out on purpose. You were down in the bathrooms when we started."

"Join us," Mandy said. "We can play Unicorns against non-Unicorns."

Elizabeth shifted her weight impatiently while Ellen and Kimberly tried to decide if they wanted to play. They had obviously washed up. They were wearing clean shorts and T-shirts and their hair was carefully combed. Finally, Kimberly took off her jacket and marched up onto the court. Ellen wasn't far behind her.

"Let's play!" Kimberly said. "I'll serve."

Of course you will, Elizabeth thought.

Kimberly didn't just tap the ball over the net either. She gave her serve everything she had left.

Elizabeth jumped up to block it. Soon the girls were playing an intense three-on-three. After a few minutes, Elizabeth was zonked. All she wanted to do was go home and plop down with a book. But she didn't want to wimp out in front of everybody. Kimberly would probably laugh in her face. And what if someone mentioned it to Sandra?

Someone else will quit soon, Elizabeth told herself.

Ellen halfheartedly hit the ball over the net. Since it was heading right for Cammi, Elizabeth didn't move. But neither did Cammi. The ball hit her squarely on the jaw before she had even noticed it coming.

"Are you OK?" Elizabeth called.

Cammi nodded, rubbing the side of her face. "It didn't hurt—much."

Elizabeth expected Cammi to say she had to go. After all, she was clearly too tired to play well. But Cammi just picked up the ball and tossed it under the net.

Ellen served again. The ball came over the net

nice and easy. Elizabeth tried to jump for the block, but her legs felt like they were made of lead. She missed.

"You guys look tired," Elizabeth said when it was her turn to serve. "Do you want to call it a night?"

Mandy stifled a yawn. "No, no—I'm fine."

"We can quit—if *you're* too tired," Kimberly said.

"What's makes you think *I'm* tired?" Elizabeth asked defensively. "I could play all night." She served. The ball went into the net.

"Hey, it's six o'clock," a lifeguard with sun-bleached hair said to the girls about ten minutes later. He was with three other guys. They all looked old enough to be in college.

"Our parents know where we are," Kimberly answered back.

The guys started to laugh.

"That's not the problem," the lifeguard called back. "The problem is that we reserved this court for six."

Mandy quickly stopped the ball. "Sorry!"

The girls hurried off the court. Elizabeth was secretly thrilled to have an excuse to go home.

"That was fun," Maria said as they staggered to their bikes.

"Definitely!" Elizabeth agreed, trying to look like she meant it.

Mandy, Maria, and Elizabeth rode most of the way home together. As Elizabeth turned her bike down her own street, all she could think about was how much her legs ached and how hungry she was. Still, Elizabeth was proud of herself for working so hard that day. The only thing that bothered her was that Sandra hadn't singled her out.

Well, tomorrow is the game, Elizabeth reminded herself. *Sandra is sure to notice how hard I'm working then.*

FOUR

"Don't be nervous," Sandra told Elizabeth and the other girls minutes before the beginning of their match on Tuesday. "As long as you remember to think like a team, everything will be fine."

The referee blew her whistle.

"Go, Sweet Valley!" Elizabeth and her teammates cheered. The team hurried onto the court. Elizabeth took her place between Maria and Ellen in the front row.

"This is it," Maria whispered.

Elizabeth nodded, taking a deep breath.

Facing them were the six players from the Weston team, all wearing blue Weston T-shirts. The team captain, who was standing in the back row, towered over the other girls. She looked about six feet tall. Elizabeth's heart started to pound. This was her team's first chance to see how they measured up to the competition. So far Elizabeth felt kind of *short*.

Elizabeth glanced into the stands, which were mostly empty. The only kids from school she saw were Grace Oliver and Winston Egbert. Jessica was at gymnastics practice.

The referee stepped foward, holding the official game ball. "Weston will serve first," she announced. The referee tossed the ball to a member of the Weston team.

The girl caught the ball—and then dropped it. "Oops," she said. The Weston team started to giggle.

Elizabeth made a face at Maria.

"They're pretty nervous," Maria whispered.

"They can't be as nervous as I am," Elizabeth whispered back.

The girl from Weston picked up the ball and served quickly.

Elizabeth took a deep breath. The ball was heading right toward her!

"Mine!" Elizabeth called out in a shaky voice. She blocked the ball neatly. Cammi, who was in the back row, set it up. Ellen spiked the ball over the net. It bounced in the sand.

Elizabeth and Maria traded surprised looks. That was easy!

"Way to go!" Sandra called from the sidelines.

Weston passed the ball under the net, and Kimberly served. The girls in Weston's front line jumped too late to stop the ball.

"Score!" Mandy yelled.

Elizabeth turned and grinned at Sandra. If they played this well in all their matches, they wouldn't just go to the California Games—they'd win the gold medal!

Kimberly put her next serve in exactly the same place as the first one. Amazingly, Weston still couldn't block it.

"Keep it up," Ellen said as she passed the ball back to Kimberly.

Kimberly did. By the time she gave up the ball, Sweet Valley was four points ahead.

Elizabeth had lost her case of the jitters—and had started enjoying herself. Every play felt just right. When it was her turn to serve, she made three points—two of them aces.

"This is fun," Maria whispered to Elizabeth as the girls were rotating positions.

"It's a dream!" Elizabeth whispered back.

"And the match goes to Team Sweet Valley," the referee said calmly about forty minutes later.

Elizabeth stepped under the net and extended her hand to the closest Weston player. "Good game," she said.

"Good game," the Weston player mumbled, looking glum.

"Good game," Elizabeth said to the Weston captain. She had to look up—*way* up—to look her in the eye.

"Good for you maybe," the other girl snarled.

Elizabeth really couldn't blame the Weston captain for being a bad sport. Sweet Valley had taken the match in straight games. If her team had lost that badly, Elizabeth would have felt grumpy too.

The referee approached Sandra and the Weston coach. "I need your signatures on the game form," she said.

"Stick around, girls!" Sandra called out. "We need to have a meeting."

Terrific, Elizabeth thought gleefully. She was sure Sandra wanted to tell them how well they'd played. *That* would be even more fun than the game had been.

As the Weston team wandered off toward their bus, Mandy skipped over to Ellen and Kimberly. "That was terrific!" she said, linking arms with her friends.

"*We* were terrific," Kimberly said with a grin.

"I feel like having a party!" Ellen exclaimed.

"A victory party," Kimberly put in, her eyes dancing. "Of course, it'll be nothing compared to the party we'll throw when we win the California Games!"

"The California Games?" Mandy repeated. "Aren't you getting a little ahead of yourself?"

"No way!" Kimberly replied. "We played like champions today! We're going to win the California Games. I can feel it!"

"Congratulations, you guys," Grace said as she and Winston joined the group.

"Thanks," Mandy said. "What did you think of the match?"

Winston made a goofy face. "It kind of made me sick to my stomach."

"Why?" Ellen demanded.

"Well, witnessing a massacre tends to make me queasy," Winston said.

Grace giggled. "Weston never had a chance."

Kimberly grinned triumphantly. "None of our opponents have a chance. We have the best coach, the best captain, and the best team. We're going straight to the California Games. And when we win there, we're going to have the biggest party Sweet Valley Middle School has ever seen!"

"Good game, you guys!" Elizabeth said as she joined Maria and Cammi on a bench near the court. She was still feeling pumped up from the game—and she couldn't wait to hear what Sandra would say about their stellar performance.

"It was a *great* game," Maria replied. She motioned toward the nearly empty stands. "I just wish more of our friends had been here to see it. Too bad Amy couldn't get out of gymnastics practice."

Elizabeth nodded. Amy Sutton was one of her best friends. "I know what you mean." Her eyes sparkled. "But look at it this way. The people who didn't show up will be that much more interested in the *Sixers* article I'm going to write!"

Elizabeth had decided to devote the upcoming *Sixers* issue to the Sweet Valley Games. She was already planning on doing an article on Jessica and the gymnastics team. And now she'd have plenty to say about the volleyball team too!

Cammi grinned. "This is so cool. You're writing an article about the team just like Sandra did about hers."

Elizabeth blushed. It *had* occurred to her that she

was doing just what Sandra had done when she was in middle school. In fact, she kind of pictured herself following in Sandra's footsteps, winning a prize for her story, and then of course going on to win the California Games. . . .

Maria swept her arms wide. "I'm picturing a full-page spread!" she exclaimed, cutting into Elizabeth's thoughts.

"Maybe we could even put it on the *front* page," Cammi suggested hopefully.

And maybe I can even do a profile of Sandra, Elizabeth added to herself. That would definitely get the coach's attention!

"You should all be proud," Sandra told the volleyball team a few minutes later. The girls were sitting in the stands facing the volleyball court. Sandra was pacing back and forth in front of them. "You played very well together today. I could almost *see* you thinking like a team. And now, you're one match closer to the California Games!"

"Yes!" Kimberly called out.

Elizabeth beamed. Winning the match had been fun. But earning Sandra's respect was even better.

"I saw some beautiful plays out there today," Sandra said, thoughtfully rubbing her stomach. "Elizabeth, you made a block in the second game that looked practically professional."

"Thanks." Elizabeth managed to keep her voice calm, but she knew her face was turning beet red with pleasure. Having Sandra notice her hard work felt fabulous.

Sandra pointed to Kimberly. "Game point, second game. Do you remember the play?"

"Sure," Kimberly said with a sniff.

"Perfect spike!" Sandra exclaimed. "You knew just where to put the ball and you got it there."

Kimberly sat up a little straighter, darting a glance at Elizabeth.

Elizabeth smiled back. She felt so good she wasn't about to let Kimberly's conceitedness get to her.

"But Kimberly couldn't have made that spike if it wasn't for Mandy," Sandra continued. "In fact, Mandy set up at least half of the points scored."

Elizabeth glanced over at Mandy. She was grinning ear to ear.

Sandra turned and smiled at Ellen. "What most impressed me about *your* game today is how much you hustled on every play," she said. "You really worked hard."

Elizabeth felt her chest tighten. She was supposed to be the hard worker, not Ellen! As far as Elizabeth was concerned, Ellen was the typical Unicorn—which meant she didn't even know the meaning of hard work.

But Ellen didn't seem to think Sandra's comment was a joke. She had a happy look on her face.

Well, maybe she was working harder than usual today, Elizabeth thought, trying to be generous. She didn't know what had gotten into her. She couldn't believe she was feeling so competitive—especially with a Unicorn.

"Maria, you played a very smart game today," Sandra went on. "You were thinking strategically and it showed."

A smart game? Elizabeth repeated to herself. *What did I play—a stupid game?* Elizabeth couldn't help but feel jealous all over again. What was one "professional block" compared to "a smart game?"

Whoa! Elizabeth told herself sternly. *I'm starting to sound like Jessica! What's going on? Maria is my friend. I shouldn't be jealous of her!*

"Cammi," Sandra went on. "Your jumping and blocking is really shaping up. I think you're getting up about two extra inches."

Elizabeth forced herself to smile at Cammi. "Good work," she whispered.

Cammi smiled shyly. "You too," she whispered back.

"You all have the right to be proud." Sandra paused for a long moment and then shook her head. "I wish I could give you a few days to enjoy your victory. But our match schedule is too tight for that. You play Big Mesa *tomorrow.* If you want to win, we're going to have to start preparing for that match *now.* Big Mesa's team is much stronger than Weston's."

"How do you know?" Ellen asked.

"Coach gossip," Sandra told her with a wink. "Big Mesa always has a powerful team. But supposedly they're extrastrong this year. You girls can't afford to make any mistakes when you play them tomorrow. Now let's talk about some fundamentals you missed in today's match."

Maria leaned toward Elizabeth. "We made mistakes?"

"I thought we were perfect," Elizabeth whispered back.

"Elizabeth," Sandra said.

Elizabeth jumped a little in her seat. "Yes?" she asked timidly.

"Sometimes you miss opportunities to spike," Sandra said, beginning to pace again. "You passed the ball twice today when you should have gone for the point. Lots of players are guilty of going for the glory too often, but you have just the opposite problem. Remember, you don't always have to let someone else score."

"OK," Elizabeth replied as steadily as she could. To her amazement, tears welled up in her eyes. *Don't be such a baby*, she ordered herself. She glanced down at her feet and blinked back her tears, but she couldn't help feeling rotten. So Sandra didn't think she had played such a great game, after all.

"As for you, Cammi," Sandra went on, "I need you to pay a little more attention on the court. Sometimes I get the idea you're watching the game, not playing it."

Elizabeth glanced up at Cammi, who was blushing furiously. Feeling a little ashamed of herself, Elizabeth breathed a sigh of relief. She did sympathize with Cammi, but at the same time she was happy Sandra was talking about someone else now.

"Kimberly," Sandra continued with a smile. "Don't forget that there's a defensive side to this game. You're great on offense, but you can't hold back for the spike on every play. If you're in the position to block, get the job done."

Kimberly turned pale.

"You need a little more power, Ellen," Sandra

went on. "When you get the opportunity to spike, don't hold back. Whomp that ball for all you're worth."

Ellen bit her lip and dropped her eyes.

Elizabeth felt Maria tense up as Sandra's gaze fell on her.

"I want to hear your voice more often, Maria," Sandra said. "Don't rely on your teammates to notice if you're open. Get into position and then let them know about it. Do what you have to do to make sure the ball gets to you." ·

Maria nodded numbly. Elizabeth thought she looked as if she'd been slapped in the face.

"Mandy, I want you to get in touch with your killer instinct," Sandra continued. "You always seem to be having fun on the court—which is great. But if you play with more mental intensity, your game will take off."

"Intensity," Mandy said, nodding gravely. "You got it."

Does Sandra think we won the game or does she think Weston lost it? Elizabeth wondered unhappily. Her good mood was completely blown. Gaining her coach's respect was going to be even harder than she'd thought.

Sandra glanced at her watch. "I can't believe how early it still is. You guys sure made quick work of Weston! Since we have time, let's finish off the day with a quick scrimmage."

Elizabeth got to her feet slowly. Her own watch told her that Sandra's rehash of the game had only been about ten minutes long. But it had felt more like ten *years*. Elizabeth didn't feel like writing about the game anymore. She could picture the headline now: Sweet Valley Wins; Wakefield Passes Too Much.

"Ellen, Maria, and Elizabeth—you can play together," Sandra suggested. "Elizabeth, why don't you serve?"

Sandra tossed the ball to Elizabeth. As Elizabeth got into position to serve, she tried to pep herself up. *Sandra didn't tell you what's wrong with your game to make you feel rotten,* she told herself. *She wanted to help you play better. That's part of being an athlete. If you can't take it, you don't belong on the court.*

"I can take it," Elizabeth whispered. She was more determined than ever to impress Sandra.

Elizabeth served the ball, whomping it as hard as she could. Kimberly had to jump about ten feet into the air in order to block it. The ball came whizzing back over the net at a difficult angle.

"I've got it!" Maria called out.

Elizabeth started to step back—out of her friend's way. But then she remembered what Sandra had said. She should go for the glory more often. So Elizabeth stepped forward and reached for the ball herself.

Maria and Elizabeth got to the ball at the same time. Their heads smacked together with a loud *whack*. Elizabeth, Maria, and the ball all landed in the sand.

"Are you two OK?" Sandra called.

"I . . . I'm fine," Elizabeth responded as she carefully

touched her head to make sure she wasn't bleeding. Actually, her head was spinning. But she didn't want Sandra to know that.

Maria scrambled to her feet. "What do you think you were doing?" she demanded sharply. "I said I had it. Didn't you hear me?"

Elizabeth felt her heart constrict. Maria had never yelled at her that way before.

"Would you guys get it together?" Ellen snapped. "Thanks to you, we're losing the scrimmage now."

"Come on, Ellen," Elizabeth said. She was about to remind Ellen that this was just a friendly practice scrimmage—not the Olympic finals. But she bit her tongue. Maybe that was the wrong attitude. Maybe great players took every game seriously.

Ellen passed the ball under the net, and Cammi served. The serve came over the net fairly slowly. Ellen spiked it right back. The ball headed toward Mandy. Mandy blocked the ball easily. Cammi set it up, and Kimberly spiked the ball at an angle that was impossible to defend.

"Nice going, Ellen," Maria said sarcastically. "If you hadn't spiked the ball immediately, maybe we could have set up a decent play."

"I'm just playing hard like Sandra," Ellen snapped back.

"Come on, you guys," Elizabeth said. "We're all on the same team here."

"Who are you to talk?" Ellen demanded nastily.

"Girls!" Sandra said warningly.

Elizabeth resisted an urge to snap back at Ellen. She knew that would only make things worse.

A few plays later, Elizabeth was about to set up Ellen, who was in a great position to spike. But then Elizabeth realized she had passed the ball on the last three plays. Would Sandra think that was too much? Probably. At the last second, Elizabeth spiked the ball herself. It flew out of bounds. Elizabeth cringed. So much for going for the glory.

Maria glared at Elizabeth. "What was that supposed to be?"

"Teamwork!" Sandra called. "Come on, girls! Think like a team!"

She must be talking to Ellen, Elizabeth told herself. After all, you couldn't go for the glory and think like a team at the same time. And Sandra definitely wanted *her* to go for the glory.

"I'm sorry we're late to pick you up," Jessica told Elizabeth a little later as the twins walked toward their mother's car. "I was so into my bar routine at gymnastics practice, I didn't notice what time it was. Mom was waiting for me for half an hour."

"That's OK," Elizabeth mumbled.

"Does anyone else need a ride home?" Jessica asked.

"No," Elizabeth said, looking down at the ground.

Jessica nudged her sister. "Aren't you even going to *ask*?"

"No," Elizabeth said firmly. She knew that if she spent another minute with any of her teammates—including Maria—she was going to go crazy. "And don't bug me about it!"

Jessica shrugged. "So, anyway, don't keep me in suspense. Did you win the—hey, what happened to your head? You're getting a huge black-and-blue mark."

Elizabeth touched her forehead. She felt a large tender spot. "Maria ran into me on the court."

"Really?" Jessica asked. "What happened?"

"I told you—Maria ran into me," Elizabeth snapped. "What else do you want to know?"

Jessica raised her eyebrows. "What's up with you?" she asked curiously. "You're almost as grouchy as Steven." Steven was the twins' fourteen-year-old brother. Elizabeth and Jessica both considered him the King of Grouches most of the time, especially when he was fighting with his sisters.

"I'm just in a bad mood, I guess," Elizabeth sighed.

"So you lost the game?" Jessica asked.

"No, we won," Elizabeth said as she climbed into the car.

Jessica looked at her sister skeptically. "You won, and you're a total grump?" She shook her head. "Sometimes it amazes me that we're twins!"

FIVE

"Hi, Elizabeth!" Amy Sutton called in the cafeteria on Wednesday.

Elizabeth waved at Amy. She carried her lunch tray over to the table where Amy and Maria were sitting. "Hi," she said as she slid into a seat.

"Hi," Maria muttered. "How's your head?"

Elizabeth reached up and touched the sore spot under her hair. "Not bad. How's yours?"

"OK, I guess," Maria sighed.

Amy raised her eyebrows. "People have been talking about your big match all day. But nobody mentioned any injuries."

"That's because this happened at practice *after* the game," Maria said.

Elizabeth shifted uncomfortably in her seat. She looked down and started to unwrap her lunch. Part of her felt like she should apologize to Maria for what had happened the day before. After all, Maria *had* called the ball. Technically, it was Elizabeth's fault they had crashed into each other. But part of Elizabeth thought apologizing was silly. She'd just been doing what Sandra told them to do: playing hard.

Amy took a sip of her juice. "So what happened? No—let me guess! You guys got into a fight with the Unicorns and they *horned* you!"

Elizabeth smiled and shook her head.

"I'll tell you what happened," Maria said bitterly. "I was getting ready to make a beautiful block when Elizabeth tackled me! I guess she thought we were playing *football*." She gave Elizabeth a dirty look. "*That's* the game where you tackle people."

Amy started to laugh, but Elizabeth couldn't bring herself to join in. She felt a little ashamed of herself—but also angry at Maria. What was she trying to imply? That Elizabeth didn't even know what game she was playing?

"You guys are so lucky," Amy said. "Playing on the team together must be a terrific experience."

Elizabeth met Maria's gaze.

"Well, it's definitely an experience," Maria said, raising her eyebrows.

But I don't know if I'd call it terrific, Elizabeth added to herself.

"I see two seats together down on the end," Jessica said. "Hurry up, Lila, grab them before someone else does."

Lila tossed her hair over her shoulder. "Fowlers do not push through crowds." She sniffed. "If you want the seats so badly, get them yourself."

Jessica rolled her eyes. Lila and Jessica had been best friends for years, but Jessica sometimes wished Lila wasn't quite so high on herself. Just because her millionaire father treated her like a princess, Lila seemed to think she was actually royalty. Jessica knew perfectly well that Lila was only pretending to be above attending the volleyball game. Practically the entire sixth grade was there. Lila wouldn't have missed a social event this important for anything.

Standing on her tiptoes, Jessica saw that Amy Sutton and Sophia Rizzo were sitting next to the empty seats. *Now if only they would look in my direction,* Jessica thought.

Jessica put two fingers in her mouth and let out a shrill whistle. Amy and Sophia turned to stare. So did practically everyone else in the stands.

"Very refined," Lila remarked with disgust.

"Save those seats for us!" Jessica hollered at Amy.

Amy rolled her eyes. "Well, since you asked so politely—"

"*Please,*" Jessica said with exaggerated politeness. Even though Amy was one of Elizabeth's best friends, she and Jessica went together about as well as sleep and slumber parties. Still, the girls spent a lot of time together. They were both members of the Boosters, the sixth-grade cheering squad. Amy was also on the gymnastics team with Jessica and Lila.

"I can't believe how many people are here," Lila said as she and Jessica squeezed through the crowd toward their seats.

"Well, what did you expect?" Jessica asked. "Everyone was talking about how the volleyball team killed Weston yesterday."

"I guess you're right," Lila said as the girls settled into their seats. "Everyone loves a winner. Hey—what's Peter DeHaven doing down there?"

Peter DeHaven, who was in the girls' class at Sweet Valley Middle School, had pulled a chair close to the court. He was aiming an expensive-looking camera at Kimberly as she warmed up.

"Elizabeth is planning to do a story on the volleyball team for the *Sixers*," Amy explained. "Peter is taking photographs to go along with it."

"Of the volleyball team?" Lila asked.

"No," Amy said dryly. "Of the men from Mars that just landed."

"Very funny." Lila turned her back on Amy. "Have you seen Peter at any of our gymnastics meets?" she asked Jessica.

"No," Jessica said. "But then again, we haven't *had* a meet yet."

"Well, I still don't think it's fair," Lila said. "Just because your sister runs the *Sixers* doesn't mean she should get to decide what the paper writes about. I think you should make her do a story on the gymnastics team."

"Fine," Jessica said with a groan. "But do you mind if we watch the game first?"

Before Lila could reply, Jessica joined in the cheer that Amy and Sophia had started. Lila sat back in her seat and folded her arms across her chest.

*   *   *

"Go, go, go!"

Elizabeth gazed up at the crowd. They were already getting rowdy—and the game hadn't even started yet.

Maria wiped her hands on her shorts. "Where did all of these people come from?" she asked Elizabeth.

"I think Kimberly had something to do with it," Elizabeth said, glancing toward where the team captain stood chatting with Ellen. "She was doing public relations for the team all day."

"Public relations?" Maria asked. "What do you mean?"

"Well, I walked by her class second period," Elizabeth began. "She was standing on her chair telling everyone who would listen about the greatest volleyball team in world history."

Maria made a face. "Yeah, right. History according to the Unicorns."

Elizabeth laughed.

"Pep-talk time!" Sandra called out.

Maria and Elizabeth walked over and joined the rest of the team. Sandra had just gotten back from filing some paperwork with the referee. Her face was flushed with excitement.

"OK, guys," Sandra said. "I know I've already told you this will be a tough game—and it will be. But you're ready for it. Just remember to think like a team, and you'll do great."

Of course we'll do great, Elizabeth thought. *We're going to win!*

*   *   *

As Elizabeth took her place facing the Big Mesa team, her confidence wavered. The Big Mesa team looked much more intimidating than Weston had. They were wearing professional-looking short black unitards with gold stripes down the sleeves. Each girl had her name embroidered on the front of her uniform. They were even wearing their hair in the same way. Elizabeth swallowed hard. Now *that* was thinking like a team!

Big Mesa served first. It wasn't a great serve, but it caught Cammi in dreamland. She jumped too late for the block. Ace.

The crowd groaned.

"I wasn't ready for that one," Cammi told Elizabeth.

Obviously not, Elizabeth thought. But she managed an encouraging smile.

Elizabeth felt herself tensing up. It seemed as though Sandra was right—Big Mesa was good. But she knew that Sandra was counting on Team Sweet Valley to play just as well, and Elizabeth was determined not to let her down.

On the next play, the Big Mesa server hit the ball to Cammi again. Elizabeth could see that Cammi misjudged the ball's angle. She jumped up too far to the right—she'd never be able to reach the ball. Elizabeth sucked in her breath. Then, at the last second, she dove for the ball and recovered it about an inch from the sand.

"Wake-field!" the crowd cheered as play continued. "Wake-field!"

Elizabeth bit back a grin. She'd gone for the

glory, all right. There was no way Sandra could have missed it!

Elizabeth exchanged triumphant smiles with her teammates. But when her eyes fell on Cammi, her grin faded. *She looks really hurt,* Elizabeth thought. But she tried to block Cammi out of her mind. *She shouldn't be hurt, anyway. The important thing is that we saved the ball. And that Sandra saw how aggressively I could play.*

On the next play, Maria was about to spike the ball when Kimberly jumped up from behind her and smashed it right between the blocker's arms.

Maria landed in the sand.

A Big Mesa player dove for the ball—and missed.

The Sweet Valley fans went wild.

But Maria was frowning. "Listen," she told Kimberly as she got to her feet. "You don't have to cover me. I can handle the balls hit to me."

"Sorry," Kimberly said with a grin.

She sure doesn't look too sorry, Elizabeth thought.

"Don't be mad," Elizabeth whispered to Maria. "Kimberly did get us possession of the ball."

"Yippee," Maria said sarcastically.

Kimberly served.

A Big Mesa player lightly tapped the ball back over the net.

Elizabeth hadn't been expecting that. She jumped too late to block the ball.

"Look alive—or get out of the way!" Maria called to Elizabeth.

Elizabeth stared at her friend. She couldn't believe

Maria was being so nasty. If that was her attitude, maybe Kimberly *should* run her down.

The referee blew her whistle. It was time for the teams to switch sides. Big Mesa was leading 0–4.

"Listen," Kimberly hissed as the girls walked around the net. "Do you want to win this game?"

"Yes," Elizabeth mumbled along with the rest of the team.

"Good," Kimberly whispered fiercely. "We can still win if you guys just stay out of my way . . . especially you," she added, pointing at Cammi.

"Kimberly!" Elizabeth exclaimed. "We're supposed to be a team!"

"We *are* a team," Kimberly whispered back. "I just happen to be the team's best player."

Elizabeth took her position, her blood boiling. Kimberly really had some nerve!

Big Mesa served the ball directly to Cammi. It was an easy block, but Cammi stepped away from the ball so that Kimberly could rush forward from the back row to stop it.

Elizabeth shook her head. *Kimberly's nasty little speech is working,* she thought. *Cammi is scared to touch the ball!*

Maria knocked the ball over the net.

Big Mesa hit it right back. Kimberly tried to block the ball, but Cammi was in her way. The ball landed in the sand—right where Kimberly *should* have been standing.

"This is great," Elizabeth overheard one of the Big Mesa players say.

"Yeah, it's awesome," another Big Mesa player

answered with a laugh. "I feel like we're playing six-on-one. No wonder we're winning!"

Yeah, Elizabeth thought, her heart sinking. *No wonder.*

"What are they doing down there?" Lila asked.

"Losing," Jessica said glumly.

Lila sighed and pulled her fingernail file out of her purse. "I can't believe you dragged me out here to watch the team lose. This isn't exactly my idea of a fun afternoon."

"It's not mine either!" Jessica snapped back. She had had just about all she could take of Lila's complaining.

"So, let's go," Lila suggested. "We still have a few hours before I have to be home for dinner. We can hit the mall."

"I can't," Jessica sighed. "I promised Elizabeth I would wait for her after the game."

Lila examined her nails, then quickly put her nail file back in her bag. "Elizabeth will understand! Like you said, everyone loves a winner. And Elizabeth is definitely a loser today."

"I'll tell Kimberly you said that," Jessica said.

"Kimberly's different." Lila smiled smugly. "Unicorns are never losers—even when they do lose. So, are you coming or not?"

"Not," Jessica said.

"Suit yourself." Lila picked up her things and left.

Jessica watched as Lila made it to the end of the row. Then Jessica stuck her tongue out at her back.

* * *

"I can't believe we lost," Ellen said loudly as the players came off the court twenty minutes later.

"Don't say it like that!" Mandy shot back.

"Like what?" Ellen asked as she pulled on her sweatshirt.

"Like it was my fault!" Mandy said.

Ellen stomped over to the first row of the stands and flopped down with a heavy sigh. "I wasn't saying it was your fault."

Mandy blushed slightly. "Oh. Sorry."

"But come to think of it, it *was* your fault," Ellen added. "At least, part your fault. You missed plenty of serves. Blocks too."

Mandy frowned. "Well, not as many as some people." She tilted her head in Cammi's direction.

"Yeah," Ellen agreed. "If you can figure out a way to get *her* off the team, let me know."

Elizabeth shot Ellen and Mandy an angry look. She was surprised that Mandy, who was usually nice, would be so mean.

"Something you wanted to say, Elizabeth?" Ellen asked in a challenging voice.

Elizabeth decided she didn't feel like picking a fight. She turned her back on Ellen and sat down next to Maria. "One win and one loss," she said sadly. "Big Mesa already has a better record than we do."

Maria made a face. "If we want to go to the California Games we'd better win our next two matches."

The Big Mesa team formed a circle on the court. "Big Mesa!" they cheered. "We're number one!"

Maria frowned in their direction. "Talk about rubbing it in."

Sandra had told the girls to hang around for a postgame wrap-up. Now as she approached them, she had a grim look on her face.

"This is going to be a bag of laughs," Maria whispered to Elizabeth.

Elizabeth nodded numbly. If Sandra's recap after the last game had been tough to hear, this one was bound to be *excruciating*.

Sandra stood quietly in front of the girls for a long moment, looking thoughtful. *Was she trying to decide what to say?* Elizabeth wondered. *Or was she giving them time to think about the game?* When Elizabeth thought about the game, the first image she had was of herself pushing Cammi out of the way so that she could get at the ball. She felt a rush of shame.

"I didn't even recognize you guys out there today," Sandra finally began in a soft voice. "Did you forget that volleyball is a team sport? Did you forget that you're supposed to be working together?"

"No," Elizabeth mumbled quietly.

"I'm not sure what it was," Sandra continued. "Maybe it was the crowd. Or maybe I gave you the wrong impression yesterday. I didn't think I needed to tell you girls this, but here it is: No one player— no matter how talented—can carry a volleyball team single-handedly. This game takes cooperation."

Elizabeth looked down at the ground. Sandra's right, she realized. Volleyball wasn't about personal glory. But she'd been so focused on impressing Sandra that she'd forgotten to work *with* her teammates.

"Do any of you have anything to say?" Sandra asked.

Elizabeth cleared her throat and tried to catch Sandra's eye. But Kimberly was slowly getting to her feet.

"Yes, Kimberly?" Sandra said.

Kimberly gave Elizabeth a meaningful look. "I just wanted to say it's hard to play like a team when *certain people* are trying to prove to a certain other person how hard they work," she said.

Elizabeth's eyes widened in horror.

"Kimberly, that's hardly the attitude we need," Sandra said with a frown. "Blaming each other won't help. What you girls need to do is figure out how you can work together." Sandra turned to Elizabeth. "Did you want to say something?" she asked.

"No," Elizabeth whispered, biting back her anger. *Who wants to be part of a team if Kimberly is on it?* she asked herself.

SIX

"Over here!" Kimberly yelled at practice the next afternoon.

Elizabeth was down on her knees in the sand, preparing to hit the ball. She had a split second to make a choice. She could pass the ball to Kimberly or hit it somewhere else. After Kimberly's comment the night before, the decision was easy to make. From her awkward position, Elizabeth hit the ball over the net.

Before Elizabeth could get back onto her feet, the ball flew right over her head and hit the sand.

"That was pitiful," Kimberly hissed at Elizabeth.

Maybe it was pitiful, Elizabeth thought. *But I'm still glad I didn't pass the ball to you.*

"Come on, guys," Sandra implored the team from the sidelines. "Think like a team!"

Team? What's that? Elizabeth wondered as she stepped into position.

Sandra stepped into the center of the court and clapped her hands for attention.

Maria caught the ball.

"I know it's early," Sandra said, brushing a stray wisp of hair off her face. "But I'm going to end practice now. I want you all to go home and relax. Try not to think—or worry—about volleyball."

Elizabeth watched as Sandra slowly made her way to her car. *Sandra never ends practice early,* she thought. Something about the way Sandra was moving made Elizabeth think she was in pain. Elizabeth felt uneasy. Was something wrong with Sandra?

"What's the matter with you people?" Mandy's angry voice broke into Elizabeth's thoughts. "I'm always open, and nobody ever passes to me! If I don't start getting the ball soon, I'm quitting!"

"Oh, like you never hog the ball!" Kimberly retorted.

"You really have no right to complain," Ellen told Mandy. "Every time you do get the ball, you spike it from eighty feet away!"

Mandy snorted. "You just wish you could spike the ball, period!"

Elizabeth watched Sandra's little red car pull out of the parking lot. She was almost certain Sandra was even *driving* more slowly than usual. "You guys," Elizabeth asked softly. "Did you think Sandra looked OK?"

"What do you mean?" Cammi asked.

"I don't know," Elizabeth said. "She seemed kind of quiet all through practice. And she looked awfully tired."

Maria rolled her eyes. "Who could blame her? Do you think listening to us fight is fun?"

"I know it isn't," Elizabeth said, shaking her head. *I just hope that's all it is,* she added to herself.

"Hey, Mandy!" Elizabeth called a few minutes later. "Wait a second!"

Mandy sighed. She was getting on her bike, which she'd just unlocked from the bike rack. *What does Elizabeth want now?* she wondered irritably. Mandy usually liked Elizabeth, but everyone on the volleyball team was bugging her. And in many ways, Elizabeth was the worst of all. She was so annoyingly understanding during all the bickering that was going on.

Elizabeth smiled at Mandy as she started to unlock her own bike. "How are the party plans coming?" she asked.

Mandy shrugged. "Pretty good, I guess. Kimberly's planning the world's biggest blowout if we win the California Games."

"That's great," Elizabeth said. "But I was talking about Sandra's shower. Have you picked a date yet?"

"Uh—not really." *Why is Elizabeth asking me all these questions?* Mandy wondered.

"What about the invitations?" Elizabeth asked.

"Are you going to buy them or make them?"

"Make them, probably," Mandy said. "I haven't really thought about it yet." *Doesn't Elizabeth think I'm good enough to plan Sandra's party?* she wondered.

"How about the present?" Elizabeth persisted. "Maybe we should make up a list of things we might like to get for her. Then we could figure out how much everyone has to contribute."

"OK," Mandy agreed with a frustrated sigh. "I'll do that."

"When?" Elizabeth asked.

"Whenever I get around to it!" Mandy snapped. "Stop nagging me!"

Elizabeth blushed. "Sorry, I didn't mean to nag. I just want to make sure Sandra has a nice shower."

"Sandra's baby isn't due for weeks," Mandy pointed out, as patiently as she could. "There's plenty of time to worry about the shower *after* we get into the California Games. Right now, I'm kind of busy with school and practices."

"If you're too busy to plan it by yourself, I'd be happy to help," Elizabeth offered. "I have lots of ideas."

"I can plan the party on my own," Mandy said, her eyes flashing. *And I definitely don't need your help!* she added to herself.

"OK," Elizabeth said. "I just thought I'd offer."

"Thanks," Mandy said firmly. "But no thanks."

"OK, no more scrimmages," Sandra told the girls at the start of practice on Friday. "I want you to lob this ball across the net. Hit it once and then rotate out. OK, let's go!"

Elizabeth looked around at her teammates. They all looked miserable—maybe because Sandra was treating them so sternly. But Elizabeth was just glad to see that Sandra was back to her energetic self.

"This is a baby drill," Maria whispered to Elizabeth. "We haven't done this since our first week."

Elizabeth shrugged and ran in for her turn. She hit the ball over the net. Kimberly missed it. Elizabeth smiled with satisfaction.

"No, *no*," Sandra said, stepping out into the court. "This is an exercise in cooperation. Hit the ball so that the other person can hit it back. The goal is to keep the ball moving."

Elizabeth picked up the ball. This time she lobbed it straight to Kimberly. But Kimberly punched it hard. She laughed when Maria couldn't hit the ball back.

"Cooperate!" Sandra called out. "You should be able to do this drill in your sleep."

Maria picked up the ball and lobbed it over the net to Cammi. But Cammi missed it.

The rest of the team groaned.

"I wasn't ready," Cammi explained meekly.

"She's never ready," Kimberly said loud enough for everyone to hear.

"You should have waited," Sandra called to Maria. "Remember, you're supposed to be working together."

"This is stupid," Maria growled as she picked up the ball. "Are you ready, Cammi?"

"Yes," Cammi replied in a miserable tone.

Maria hit the ball over the net very softly. Cammi returned it. And the ball actually stayed in the air until Elizabeth hit it to Kimberly. Elizabeth's shot was off slightly, but Kimberly didn't move to the side to get it. Instead, she put her hands on her hips and watched the ball hit the sand.

"You're supposed to hit it *to* me," Kimberly told Elizabeth.

"I *tried*," Elizabeth snapped back. "You could have gotten it if you had just moved a few inches."

Kimberly stomped her foot. "You have rotten aim!"

"Oh, yeah?" Elizabeth replied. "Well—you're lazy!"

"Come on, girls," Sandra called out. "Let's try it again."

"Do we have to?" Kimberly whined. "This isn't teaching us anything we don't already know."

"Stop complaining!" Elizabeth called to her.

Kimberly's eyes widened in shock. "Don't you dare tell me what to do!" she yelled back. "I'm the captain of this team. Not you!"

Elizabeth was so angry she could feel the blood pounding in her ears. Why did Kimberly insist on acting so stupid? Didn't she know they were on the same team?

"Why do you keep picking on me?" Elizabeth demanded.

"Because you ask for it!" Kimberly yelled.

"Girls!" Sandra came toward them. "Please . . ." Elizabeth frowned in confusion as Sandra gasped and slid to the ground. Her eyes rolled back in her head, and then she went completely limp.

SEVEN

For a long moment, nobody moved.

Elizabeth stared at Sandra lying motionless in the sand. She was so surprised, she couldn't even think.

"Oh my gosh," Ellen breathed.

Cammi put her hand to her mouth in horror. "Is she alive?" she whispered.

Elizabeth knelt down next to Sandra on the sand. Sandra's eyes were closed and Elizabeth could barely see her breathing. Her skin was an unnatural gray color.

"She's alive," Elizabeth said with relief. "But I think she needs help."

"Do you think she's having her baby?" Mandy asked.

"On the beach?" Kimberly demanded. "No way!"

"And she's not due for two months," Cammi added.

"I don't think that's it," Elizabeth said. She had listened to her mother describe her labor with the twins often enough to know this was not how it was supposed to happen. Mrs. Wakefield's story involved packing to go to the hospital and hours of waiting. She had never mentioned passing out cold.

"OK, everyone," Kimberly suddenly yelled. "Listen to me!"

"Shut up, Kimberly," Mandy siad. "We don't need you're I'm-the-team-captain act now. This is an emergency!"

Kimberly's face flushed a brilliant red. She crossed her arms over her chest and marched off toward the stands.

"What do you think we should do?" Mandy asked Elizabeth.

Elizabeth looked up at her teammates, who were standing above her in a circle—waiting for her to say something. But she had no idea what to do. She was so scared she couldn't think straight.

"Well, I . . ." Elizabeth stopped and took a deep breath to calm herself. "I'm sure my mother would know what to do," she continued in an agonized voice. "Maybe I should go call her."

"You stay with Sandra," Ellen said quickly. "I'll go call my mom."

"No, I will!" Cammi said.

"My house is closest to the beach," Mandy argued. "I'll call!"

Elizabeth watched as the three girls all ran off in separate directions. She and Maria exchanged concerned looks. Then Elizabeth looked down at Sandra's pale face.

"Please hurry," she whispered.

Where is Mom right now? Mandy asked herself as she ran toward the pay phone near the rest rooms on the beach. *Work?* No, this was one of her days off. *Maybe she's at some volunteer thing. But what? PTA? The museum?* No, no, Mandy decided. *Neither of them met on Friday afternoon.*

It was Friday! The message finally got through to Mandy's confused brain. Her family always had dinner together on Friday. And since her mother had Fridays off, she indulged in her love of cooking. Mandy's mother could be found in only one place on Friday afternoon. In her kitchen. Cooking.

Mandy sprinted up to the pay phone and put in a quarter. The phone at her house rang once. Twice. Three times.

"Hi, you've reached the Millers!" Mandy was listening to her own cheerful voice. "Please leave a message at the beep."

Mandy hung up the phone in defeat. Actually, there were two places her mother could be found on Friday afternoons. In her kitchen or at the grocery store, picking up some last-minute ingredients.

*   *   *

Cammi raced across the sand toward the pay phone in the parking lot. A teenaged girl in a bright red bikini was talking on it. "Let's meet at the mall," she was saying as Cammi ran up.

"Excuse me," Cammi said softly. "I really need to use the phone."

The girl frowned at Cammi and turned her back. "How about in front of the movie theater?" she said.

Cammi took a deep breath and tried to calm down. It sounded as if the girl's conversation was almost over. Cammi crossed her fingers and closed her eyes. "Please let Sandra be OK," she whispered softly.

"No, I don't want to meet in front of Shoe Works," the girl said loudly into the phone. "You know Pete works there. And I have no desire to see him ever again. I've told you that at least five times. How about in the food court?"

Cammi sighed impatiently and marched around the phone so that she was facing the girl. "I have to make a very important call," she said as loudly as she dared.

"It's nothing, Marci," the girl said into the phone. "Just some kid bugging me for the phone."

Cammi felt her anger growing. "I'm bugging you because it's an emergency!" she yelled, stomping her foot. "Now just tell Marci you'll meet her at the movie theater and hang up!"

The girls' eyes widened. But she did exactly what Cammi said. "You ought to calm down, kid," she said as she walked off. "You're going to have a heart attack before you're a teenager."

A heart attack, Cammi thought, her panic rising. *Could that be what's wrong with Sandra?*

Cammi's hands were shaking as she picked up the phone. At the same time, she fished inside her pocket for change, but she couldn't feel any. Cammi put the phone down and turned her pockets inside out. Except for a little lint, they were both completely empty.

Ellen skidded up to the phone booth outside the snack bar. She quickly slipped a coin into the slot and punched in her home phone number.

"Bill's Auto Shop," came a gruff voice.

"Bill's what?" Ellen asked, confused.

"Auto Shop," the voice repeated. "We're your one-stop shop for all of your auto needs. How may I help you today?"

"You can't—" Ellen said quickly. "I must have dialed the wrong number. I can't even drive yet!"

"Well, call us when you can," the man said with a chuckle.

How could I have dialed the wrong number? Ellen wondered as she quickly hung up the phone. She'd had the same number since she was a baby. Her mother had made her memorize it in case she got lost on the way home from *kindergarten.* How could she forget it now—when Sandra was counting on her?

Think! Ellen ordered herself. She took ten slow breaths. She didn't dial until she was absolutely certain she had the right number.

"Hello? Bill's Auto Shop," came the same gruff voice.

Ellen let out a strangled noise. She quickly hung up the phone.

It's OK, Ellen told herself. *I'll just call information and get my home number.*

"But what's the number for information?" Ellen asked out loud. She couldn't remember it. But then she did remember something important: The number for information was always printed on the telephone.

Ellen peered at the phone more closely. But the little card with the numbers on it was gone. Where it should have been, someone had written "Joanie Loves Bob" in hot pink nail polish.

"What's taking them so long?" Maria asked impatiently.

Elizabeth glanced at her watch for what seemed like the hundredth time. Mandy, Cammi, and Ellen had already been gone for five minutes. Elizabeth scanned the beach. There was still no sign of them.

Sandra's condition hadn't changed either. Except for a few moans and garbled words, she hadn't said anything. And she hadn't moved. But she was still breathing. Elizabeth was keeping a careful eye on that.

Elizabeth kept wishing someone would walk by. Someone responsible—like a doctor. But it was an unusually gray day in Sweet Valley. The beach was practically deserted.

"I think we should go for help ourselves," Kimberly said in a tight voice. She had crept back onto the court as soon as Mandy had run off. Now she was sitting on the sand next to Sandra, a worried frown on her face.

"But the others are already calling. . . ." Elizabeth pointed out.

"Well, let's get a lifeguard," Kimberly suggested. "They're all trained in first aid. They'll know what to do."

Elizabeth slapped her forehead. *Why didn't I think of a lifeguard?* she wondered. She almost felt like hugging Kimberly. Instead, she jumped to her feet. "I'll go!"

"I'll come with you," Maria said. "Are you OK here by yourself?"

Kimberly nodded.

Elizabeth and Maria took off across the sand toward the water.

"The closest tower is over there!" Maria said, pointing.

Elizabeth sprinted after Maria toward the tower, where a lifeguard usually sat surveying the water. But the beach wasn't usually this empty. *Please let someone be on duty,* Elizabeth thought desperately.

When the girls got to the tower, a woman in an official orange lifeguard's bathing suit was just climbing off the tower. She quickly took in the girls' panicked faces. "What's wrong?" she asked with concern.

Elizabeth was so out of breath, she could hardly speak. "Our coach—" she started.

"She's pregnant—" Maria said.

"Passed out—" Elizabeth said.

"Volleyball court—" Maria said, pointing.

"Does she need an ambulance?" the lifeguard demanded.

"Yes!" Maria and Elizabeth shouted together.

The lifeguard pulled a walkie-talkie off a stand on the tower and immediately began talking into it.

Maria and Elizabeth traded relieved looks.

The lifeguard clicked off the walkie-talkie and tucked it into her first aid kit. "Let's go!" she exclaimed.

Minutes later, an ambulance, its siren blaring, pulled into the parking lot next to the volleyball court. A man and a woman in green uniforms immediately jumped out of the cab and ran toward Sandra. A third worker hopped out of the back of the ambulance, pulling a stretcher after her. She left the back door open.

Elizabeth and Maria stepped back as the emergency medical service workers began to examine Sandra.

"Do you think she's going to be OK?" Maria whispered to Elizabeth.

Elizabeth shrugged. She was afraid if she tried to talk, she would start to cry. The workers were leaning over Sandra, so Elizabeth couldn't see what was going on.

"All right, let's load her!" one of the EMS workers called. Working together, the EMS workers lifted Sandra onto the stretcher. Then they picked up the stretcher and began trotting toward the ambulance.

"Move it!" one of the workers barked at

Kimberly, who didn't get out of the way fast enough. "Seconds count here!"

Kimberly jumped to one side.

The workers loaded Sandra into the back of the ambulance. They jumped in and zoomed off, the ambulance's siren screaming.

The girls stood together, watching as the ambulance disappeared. *Seconds count,* Elizabeth repeated to herself. She couldn't help wondering how many seconds they had wasted.

EIGHT

"Mmm, yummy," Jessica said to Elizabeth the next morning. "Soggy cereal is the best, isn't it?"

Elizabeth glanced at the bowl of Corny O's that had been sitting in front of her for the last ten minutes. The cereal was turning into mush.

"I'm not very hungry," Elizabeth explained.

Jessica felt like groaning. Elizabeth had been moping ever since she got home from volleyball practice the afternoon before. Jessica knew Elizabeth was worried about her coach, who'd had some kind of fit. But in her opinion, Elizabeth had moped enough. Her long face was starting to get on Jessica's nerves.

Jessica smiled brightly, prepared to cheer Elizabeth up. "Guess what happened at gymnastics yesterday?" she asked, sitting down across from Elizabeth at the table.

"What?" Elizabeth asked without much interest.

"Well, Lila was working on the beam, and . . ." Jessica broke off and frowned. Elizabeth didn't seem to be listening. She was moodily tracing the pattern on the tablecloth, apparently lost in thought.

"Elizabeth, are you listening to me?" Jessica demanded.

Elizabeth glanced up quickly. "What? Oh, yeah. I'm listening."

Jessica sighed. "Well, anyway, Lila's feet were slippery for some reason. And when she got to the end of the beam, she lost her balance. She fell off the beam completely out of control."

"Oh. Is she OK?" Elizabeth asked, swishing her cereal around in her bowl.

Jessica rolled her eyes. "She's fine. That's the funny part. While she was in the air, she did a somersault and landed on her feet! A perfect dismount. Only Lila will never be able to do it again. It's way beyond her ability."

"That's nice," Elizabeth said in a monotone. Then she got up and put her bowl in the sink.

"It's not nice!" Jessica exploded. "It's funny. Can't you even crack a smile?"

Elizabeth sighed. "I'm sorry, Jess. I guess I'm a little distracted. I'm just wondering about how Sandra's doing."

Jessica got up and marched over to the wall phone. "There's only one way to find out," she said, pulling out the phone book.

"What are you doing?" Elizabeth demanded.

"Calling the hospital," Jessica said calmly. "You

can call and get information on patients' conditions, you know."

"I know." Elizabeth bit her lip. "But please don't call."

"Why not?" Jessica demanded.

"Because I'm scared," Elizabeth whispered. "What if something horrible happened?"

"Then at least you'll know," Jessica said as patiently as she could.

"I don't want you to call," Elizabeth said firmly.

Jessica sighed. "Then go down to the hospital and find out for yourself."

"Will you come with me?" Elizabeth asked softly.

Suddenly, Jessica felt sorry for Elizabeth. She really did sound scared. Jessica walked across the kitchen and gave her sister a hug.

"I wish I could come," Jessica said quietly. "But I have gymnastics practice all afternoon. Want to wait until this evening?"

Elizabeth took a deep breath, then slowly shook her head. "I can't wait that long. I think I'll go alone."

Elizabeth forced herself to march up to the nurses' station. She had stopped at the florist on the way to the hospital and was carrying a bouquet of irises and yellow tulips. Her heart was pounding so loudly she was sure the nurse would be able to hear it. But apparently, she couldn't. She didn't even look up as Elizabeth approached.

"Excuse me," Elizabeth whispered.

The nurse glanced up from her computer long

enough to smile at Elizabeth. "Hi. May I help you?"

"Can you tell me how to find a patient?" Elizabeth asked.

"Sure," the nurse said. "Who are you here to see?"

"Sandra Kimbali," Elizabeth replied.

The nurse hit a few keys on her computer and then frowned. "There were some complications with Mrs. Kimbali's delivery," the nurse said. "You need to go to the special care nursery."

"Delivery?" Elizabeth repeated. "But Sandra wasn't supposed to have her baby for two months!"

"That's probably why he's in special care," the nurse said.

He, Elizabeth thought as she walked down the hallway in the direction the nurse had pointed out. *Sandra had her baby—and it's a boy.* For a moment, Elizabeth's heart leaped up at the wonder of it all. Yesterday this little person hadn't existed. It was amazing! But as she continued down the hallway, Elizabeth felt the panic rising in her throat. Special care nursery? That didn't sound good.

"You look lost," the nurse on duty in the special care nursery greeted Elizabeth. "May I help you find someone?"

Elizabeth took a deep breath. "Sandra Kimbali."

This nurse didn't have to type Sandra's name into the computer. "Mrs. Kimbali is one of our most popular patients," she said with a laugh. "But I'm afraid you can't see her."

Elizabeth's eyes widened. "Why not?" she whispered, fearing the worst.

"Don't worry, Mrs. Kimbali is going to be fine," the nurse replied gently. "But as long as she's in special care, only her immediate family can visit."

"Oh," Elizabeth said. She was bummed out that she couldn't see Sandra, but more than anything, she was relieved. Sandra was going to be OK! She held out the flowers. "Do you think you could give her these? My name's on the card."

The nurse smiled and took the bouquet. "I'm sure Mrs. Kimbali will be delighted you brought these for her."

The nurse turned back to her work. But Elizabeth didn't budge. There was one more thing she had to ask.

"Excuse me," Elizabeth said. "But can you tell me how Sandra's baby is?"

The nurse looked up. "Well, his lungs are very weak," she replied calmly. "We're doing everything we can for him."

"But he *is* going to make it, right?" Elizabeth asked.

The nurse gave her a sympathetic smile. "We don't know yet."

Elizabeth's throat tightened with unshed tears. *Poor Sandra,* she thought sadly. *She must be so worried.*

"If you'd like to see the baby, you can peek in the window of the nursery on your way out," the nurse said kindly. "It's right down that hallway."

"Thank you," Elizabeth whispered. She crept down the hallway, her heart thumping. How would seeing the baby make her feel?

As Elizabeth approached the window, she was

surprised to see that Mandy was already there.

"Hi," Elizabeth said uneasily as she joined Mandy at the window, remembering that the last time they had seen each other, things had been pretty tense.

"Hi," Mandy whispered. "Isn't he adorable?"

Elizabeth's eyes followed Mandy's gaze toward an incubator marked "Christopher Kimbali." Inside was an impossibly tiny baby on a blue receiving blanket. Elizabeth's heart ached as she watched Christopher stretch his teeny face into a yawn. He *was* adorable.

Mandy nudged Elizabeth when a man came into the nursery. He had a doctor's scrub suit tied on over his clothes and a surgical mask on over a thick reddish beard. The man exchanged a few words with the nurse on duty and then walked over to Christopher's incubator. "That must be Sandra's husband," Mandy whispered.

"Maybe we should leave them alone," Elizabeth suggested.

Mandy nodded and the two girls started to tiptoe away.

"Isn't Christopher cute?" Mandy asked as they reached the door to the steps. "He's so tiny."

Elizabeth nodded. "I just hope he—" Her voice caught and she took a deep breath. "I hope he makes it."

Mandy put her hand on Elizabeth's arm. "Try to think positively," she said. "Doctors can do amazing things sometimes."

Elizabeth met Mandy's gaze. Not long ago, Mandy had been sick with cancer, and she'd spent months in the hospital herself. But with her doctor's help, she'd recovered. In fact, Mandy seemed so strong and healthy, Elizabeth could hardly believe she'd ever been sick.

Now, Elizabeth could only hope that Christopher would be as lucky as Mandy.

NINE

I thought the weekend would never end, Elizabeth said to herself as she spun her locker combination on Monday morning. Normally, Elizabeth enjoyed having a break from school. But this weekend had been torture. She had spent both days worrying about Sandra and her baby. She was pretty much thrilled to be back at school, where she could focus on her classes and her friends.

But as Elizabeth joined the rush toward class, she felt her stomach make a nervous lurch. Ellen and Kimberly were walking down the hall toward her, and all at once, Elizabeth remembered how nasty things had gotten on the volleyball team. She drew in her breath, expecting Ellen and Kimberly to snub her.

But as Ellen and Kimberly came closer, Elizabeth saw that they looked almost glad to see her.

"Hey," Kimberly said.

"How's it going?" Ellen added as they passed.

Elizabeth tried not to look too surprised. "Hi. OK, I guess."

She moved down the hallway, feeling both relieved and confused. *I haven't seen them act that friendly in ages,* she thought. Could what happened to Sandra actually have had a good effect on the team?

Then Elizabeth's heart dropped. *What* team? Even with Sandra's coaching, Team Sweet Valley was turning into one big backbiting mess. But without her? Elizabeth shuddered. Would she have to kiss her dreams of going to the California Games good-bye?

"Hi," Maria said to Elizabeth that morning in math class. "Do you mind if I sit here?"

"Of course not!" Elizabeth said. Maria always sat next to her in math, but Elizabeth was thrilled that her friend wanted to today. She hadn't seen or spoken to Maria since Friday afternoon. And they hadn't exactly been getting along well then. Elizabeth wouldn't have been too surprised if Maria had wanted to sit as far away from her as possible.

"How was your weekend?" Elizabeth asked Maria.

"Miserable," Maria mumbled as she took out her books.

Elizabeth didn't need her friend to explain. "Mine too," she sighed. For a moment she sat staring at her homework, but she couldn't focus. Finally, she said what she was thinking out loud. "What do you think is going to happen to the volleyball team now?" she asked Maria.

Maria shrugged. "I have no idea."

Mrs. Wyler stood up then and cleared her throat. "OK, kids, let's get started." As Mrs. Wyler started to write equations on the board, Elizabeth tried to concentrate, but her mind kept drifting. She thought about the tiny little boy in an incubator at Sweet Valley Hospital, and about Sandra, and about the volleyball team. The team was supposed to practice that afternoon. Would anyone even show up?

"How's that article on the volleyball team coming?" Mr. Bowman asked Elizabeth at lunchtime. Mr. Bowman was Elizabeth's English teacher and the faculty adviser to the *Sixers*. Elizabeth was spending part of her lunch period in his classroom, catching up on some work for the newspaper.

Elizabeth glanced up at Mr. Bowman, feeling guilty. "I've been meaning to talk to you about that," she said. "The truth is it's not coming along well at all."

Mr. Bowman pulled a chair up to the desk where Elizabeth was working. "Is it a reporting problem or a writing problem?" he asked.

Elizabeth sighed. "Actually, it's a volleyball problem."

Mr. Bowman raised his eyebrows and smiled. "Well, I'm not sure I can help you with that. But you can try me, if you like."

Elizabeth let her breath out all at once. "Well, to begin with our coach—her name is Sandra—is in the hospital."

"That sounds serious," Mr. Bowman said.

"It is," Elizabeth confirmed. "She had a baby— but *weeks* before she should have. The baby is really tiny. And the nurses say he might not make it."

Mr. Bowman's forehead wrinkled with concern. "I'm sure you and your teammates must be very worried about your coach and her baby. But that shouldn't stop you from competing. I don't know Sandra, but I'm sure she'd want you to go ahead with your matches."

"I'm not sure we can," Elizabeth admitted. "I don't know why, but lately the team hasn't done anything but fight. We're not really much of a team anymore at all. Sandra was pretty much the only thing that was holding us together."

Mr. Bowman gave Elizabeth a reassuring smile. "I'll bet you can think of a way to rally your teammates. After all, Elizabeth, you have a lot of experience working with a team."

"I do?" Elizabeth asked. She was beginning to think Mr. Bowman had confused her with someone else. She hadn't been on a team since she'd played soccer in grade school.

"Of course," Mr. Bowman said. "What else would you call the *Sixers* staff?"

Elizabeth frowned. "Well, yeah, but that's different."

"Not different at all," Mr. Bowman argued. "You have to deal with a lot of conflicting views and personalities, don't you?"

Elizabeth's lips curled in a small smile. "I guess so," she admitted.

"Don't give up, Elizabeth," Mr. Bowman told her. "I'm sure you and your teammates will work something out."

"Thanks, Mr. Bowman," Elizabeth said. She felt

a little more hopeful. Mr. Bowman was a pretty smart guy. If he thought things would work out, maybe they really would.

Later that afternoon Elizabeth sat alone on the beach near the volleyball court. Even after Mr. Bowman's pep talk she hadn't had the nerve to ask the other girls if they were planning to show up.

"Please let them come," Elizabeth whispered to herself.

If they didn't show up, the season was over. Elizabeth thought about the California Games. She'd never realized how much she had wanted to go until her chance started to slip away. It would have been one thing if the team hadn't qualified. But not making it because the team had fallen apart was much harder to take.

"Hi, Elizabeth."

Elizabeth glanced up and saw Maria standing above her. Elizabeth's heart leaped. At least she wasn't the only one to show up. "I'm glad you're here," she told Maria.

"Thanks," Maria said, sitting in the sand beside Elizabeth. "But if we want to play, *everyone* has to show."

Elizabeth sighed. Maria was right. *All* of their teammates had to play in order for Team Sweet Valley to compete.

"Hi, you guys," came a soft voice.

Elizabeth looked over her shoulder to find Cammi standing over them, looking awkward and·shy.

"Hi, Cammi!" Elizabeth said warmly.

"I'm glad you came," Maria added.

Cammi smiled as she joined the other girls in the sand. "I wasn't sure whether I *should* come," she said. "This was kind of a last-minute decision."

"Now all we need are the Unicorns," Maria said solemnly.

Elizabeth couldn't help but giggle. "I never thought I'd hear you say *that*," she told Maria.

"Everyone's here!" Elizabeth announced triumphantly when she spotted Mandy jogging up to the court a few minutes later. Ellen and Kimberly had already arrived.

"That's great," Maria said. "But we still don't have a coach."

Elizabeth bit her lip. "Did you bring your ball?" she asked Maria.

Maria shook her head. "I didn't think of it."

"Maybe we should just go home," Kimberly said with a shrug. "What can we do here alone?"

"Nothing," Ellen said firmly.

Elizabeth let out all her breath in a rush. She knew her teammates wanted to play—if they hadn't they wouldn't have bothered to show up. She couldn't let them give up so easily. "Come on, you guys," she said uncertainly. "We can—"

Elizabeth broke off as a van pulled up. Mr. Caldwell, the swimming coach, was behind the wheel. He stopped the van and waved. Then he hopped out, hauling a mesh bag of volleyballs after him.

"Hi, girls!" Mr. Caldwell said, trotting toward them. "Sorry to be late."

Elizabeth gave him a baffled smile. "That's OK."

"Are you going to be our new coach?" Ellen asked.

Mr. Caldwell looked startled. "Well, yes, but only temporarily," he said. "The truth is, I don't know a thing about volleyball. Even if I did, I have to be at the pool in just a few minutes. So I'm afraid you girls are on your own for practices. The best I can do is show up at games and deal with the official mumbo jumbo."

Elizabeth and Maria traded looks.

"You mean, *nobody* is going to be here for our practices?" Mandy asked.

"No," Mr. Caldwell said. "But I'm sure everything will work out fine. I spoke to Mrs. Kimbali today and she told me you guys work *great* together. Gotta run!" With a bright smile and a wave, he climbed back into the van.

Elizabeth silently shook her head as Mr. Caldwell drove off.

Is he kidding? she thought. *We work great together?* Nothing could be more ridiculous.

For a moment, Elizabeth felt like giving up. But then she remembered what Mr. Bowman said about teamwork. And she thought about how much she wanted to go to the California Games. Slowly, she reached for the balls.

"OK, team," Elizabeth said, stressing the last word ever so slightly. "What's our schedule look like this week?"

"Well, game tomorrow," Maria said. "Game Wednesday. Final qualifier on Friday."

Elizabeth took a deep breath. "All right," she said, looking around the circle at her teammates. "Hands up if you want to win those games. Hands up if you want to win them for Sandra. And for baby Christopher."

Slowly, all around the circle, hands went up. Elizabeth wondered if the other girls were wondering what she was wondering: Had they somehow caused Sandra's early delivery by making her life miserable? If they had been working together on the beach when Sandra first collapsed, would the time saved have made a difference? But Elizabeth pushed those thoughts out of her mind. "Let's get to work!"

Kimberly stepped forward and pulled the ball out of Elizabeth's hands. "We'll get started when I say so," she said in a prickly voice. "Don't forget that I'm the team captain."

Before Elizabeth could reply, Mandy spoke up. "Come on, Kimberly," she said. "It doesn't matter who's in charge."

Kimberly glared at Mandy, her hands on her hips. "What do you mean it doesn't—"

"We're doing this for Sandra, remember?" Mandy continued patiently.

Kimberly held Mandy's gaze for an instant longer. Elizabeth's heart thudded as she wondered whether Kimberly would storm off, clutching the ball. But instead Kimberly tossed the ball to her.

"For Sandra," Kimberly agreed in a tight voice.

"Let's scrimmage," Kimberly said as the girls gathered on the court after stretching out. She shot

Elizabeth a look—as if challenging her to disagree.

"Fine," Elizabeth said evenly.

"I'll play with you," Ellen told Kimberly.

"Me too," Mandy put in.

Great, Elizabeth thought as she followed Maria and Cammi around the net. *Unicorns against non-Unicorns. So much for thinking like a team.*

Kimberly served. The first few volleys went well. But then Ellen rocketed the ball over the net from the back line. Elizabeth's team returned the ball. But Kimberly stepped back and let it hit the sand.

"What are you doing?" Ellen demanded.

Kimberly took a deep breath. "Stopping the scrimmage," she said calmly. "I just wanted to say that was a bad play. Ellen, you hit the ball right to Maria. I probably couldn't have stopped their return even if I'd tried. If this had been a real game, we would have just lost a point."

Elizabeth, along with the other girls, turned to look at Ellen, who was turning bright red.

"You're right," Ellen admitted finally. "Sandra wouldn't have liked that play."

"Let's remember to work together—for Sandra," Kimberly said. "You guys can take the next serve."

As Cammi got ready to serve, Elizabeth caught Kimberly's eye and smiled at her. Maybe she wasn't so bad after all.

On the next play, Ellen set up the ball for Mandy. Mandy smashed the ball so hard, Elizabeth, Cammi, and Maria couldn't come close to it. But Elizabeth didn't mind.

"That was a beautiful play!" Elizabeth called out.

"Yeah," Maria said. "Great spike, Mandy!"

"I couldn't have done it without that graceful setup." Maria bowed to Ellen.

"It was my sincere pleasure," Ellen said in a snooty old lady's voice.

Cammi rolled her eyes and laughed. "All right, you guys. Enough of the mutual admiration society. Let's get to work!"

On the next play, Mandy spiked the ball again. But this time Elizabeth was ready for it. She neatly blocked the ball, then Cammi stepped forward to set it up, and Maria spiked it over the net.

Kimberly dove for the ball, but she didn't get to it in time.

"Nice one, Elizabeth!" Mandy called out.

"Sandra would have liked *that* play." Cammi's voice sounded wistful.

Elizabeth knew how Cammi felt. Even though everyone was finally working together, Elizabeth still missed Sandra. It was hard not to think about her.

The girls began to play again. A few plays later, Kimberly got in a good spike. Cammi went for the ball.

But Maria jumped in front of Cammi in a wild attempt to block. They both missed the ball.

Elizabeth frowned as Maria rose to her feet. She felt like scolding her friend—Maria was falling back into her old habits. But Elizabeth forced herself to stay quiet.

Maria slowly looked around at her silent teammates. Then she held a hand out to Cammi. "Sorry," she said softly, helping Cammi up. "You might have gotten that if I hadn't been in the way."

Elizabeth bit back a smile. Her teammates really *were* on their best behavior. But even so, she couldn't help feeling a little sad. She wished everyone could have behaved this well when Sandra was there.

On her way home from practice, Elizabeth stopped her bike outside a store called *Lullaby Land* in downtown Sweet Valley.

Elizabeth didn't want to bug Mandy anymore about the shower for Sandra—she didn't want to risk causing more tension, especially now that the team seemed to be pulling itself together. But now that Christopher had been born, Elizabeth decided it was time to buy him a present. She had never bought a baby gift before, so she didn't know many stores that sold baby things. She chose *Lullaby Land* because it was on her way home.

As she stepped into the shop, Elizabeth was suddenly aware of her grubby workout clothes and dirty hands. The store looked more like a museum than like a place to buy a teddy bear. Most of the merchandise was displayed in big oak cases. As Elizabeth walked by the cases, she felt someone following her. She glanced back and saw an elderly man dressed in a neat three-piece suit.

"May I help you?" the man asked, bowing slightly.

"I'm looking for a baby gift . . ." Elizabeth's voice trailed off when she noticed that her shoes were leaving tracks on the plush white carpeting.

"We have lots of lovely things," the man began.

"Is there anything in particular you had in mind?"

"Well . . . may I see that bib please?" Elizabeth pointed to the first thing she noticed. Anything to keep the shopkeeper from seeing the marks she made.

"Very well," the shopkeeper said, stepping behind the counter. He used a key to open the case and pulled out the bib. Elizabeth didn't have much experience with babies, but she knew that this was an unusual bib. It was made of crushed maroon velvet. A double row of white lace decorated the edges. Elizabeth flipped it over and noticed a tag that read "Dry Clean Only." She also noticed the price tag: $24.

Elizabeth quickly pushed the bib toward the shopkeeper. "Do you have anything more—practical?"

The shopkeeper raised his bushy eyebrows. "Well—"

"How about one of those cute little overall outfits?" Elizabeth suggested.

"I really don't think you'd be interested in those." The shopkeeper sniffed.

"I wouldn't?" Elizabeth asked curiously.

The shopkeeper leaned toward her over the counter. He glanced over his shoulder—even though they were alone in the shop. "The least expensive outfit is over forty dollars," he whispered discreetly.

Elizabeth felt her face heating up. "That *is* too much," she admitted sheepishly. "How about a stuffed animal?"

"Over there," the shopkeeper said, bowing in the direction of the display case. "But I don't think you'll—like them."

I'm sure there's something *I'll like,* Elizabeth

thought as she walked across the store to examine the display of stuffed animals. She picked up a smallish zebra. Its fur was incredibly soft, and Elizabeth instantly fell in love with it. She picked up a tiny tag attached to one of the zebra's legs. It read $42! Elizabeth quickly put the zebra down, and picked up the smallest animal on the shelf. It was $36. Elizabeth sighed. She'd never guessed baby presents were so expensive!

Elizabeth was beginning to wish she had just gone to the mall. As she turned away from the stuffed animals, she saw that the shopkeeper was lying something out on top of the case. Curious, Elizabeth walked over to him.

The shopkeeper had put out a row of fuzzy rattles. Each one had a handle in the shape of a different animal.

"How cute!" Elizabeth exclaimed. "How much is the bunny one?"

The shopkeeper made a face. "Well, you understand they are made of plastic," he said dismissively.

Elizabeth nodded impatiently. "So—how much?"

"The craftsmanship is not first-rate," the shopkeeper added.

Elizabeth shrugged. "I don't think the baby will mind!"

The shopkeeper sighed. "Well, if you insist— they're three dollars."

Elizabeth beamed. That was more like it. And in her opinion, an animal rattle was cuter than a velvet bib, anyway. "I'll take one!" she exclaimed.

This time Kimberly smiled. Elizabeth started to relax. Maybe this wasn't going to be so bad after all.

"What's going on?" Mr. Caldwell asked as the girls ran off the court forty minutes later. "Is the game over already?"

Kimberly burst out laughing. "The game *and* the match. Weren't you watching?"

"Yes," Mr. Caldwell said. "But Sandra told me a match was three games. You've only played two games, right?"

Ellen put a hand on Mr. Caldwell's arm. "Yes. But we won both of them."

Mr. Caldwell smiled. "I get it. Even if the other team won the next game, they couldn't win. So you don't have to play that game, right?"

"Um—right," Elizabeth said. She was thinking about something Mr. Caldwell had said. *Sandra told me. . . .* That had to mean that Mr. Caldwell had talked to Sandra since she went into the hospital.

"Mr. Caldwell," Elizabeth asked softly. "What else did Sandra say? Is she OK?"

Mr. Caldwell sighed. "Yes, Sandra is fine."

Kimberly and Ellen stopped chatting about the game and stepped closer to Mr. Caldwell.

"What about the baby?" Mandy whispered.

"Sandra told me there's been no change in his condition," he said sadly.

No change, Elizabeth repeated to herself. "Um, is that good or bad news?" she asked timidly.

Mr. Caldwell shrugged. "It's anybody's guess."

*   *   *

"Heads up, Cammi!" Elizabeth called to her on Wednesday.

Cammi looked up—just in time to get hit by the ball.

Elizabeth groaned.

Team Sweet Valley was in the middle of their first game against Cedar Springs. Cedar Springs was winning 11–2.

"If only we could get a chance to serve," Maria said in frustration.

"First we have to get a ball past their defense," Elizabeth responded.

"I know that!" Maria snapped.

"Sorry," Elizabeth said quickly. She was determined not to take Maria's tone personally. She knew it was the game that was stressing her friend out. She felt tense herself.

On the next play, Kimberly spiked the ball hard. Unfortunately, it sailed right to Cedar Springs' best blocker.

"That's OK," Elizabeth said to Kimberly. "We'll get them."

When the ball came whizzing back over the net, Elizabeth managed to block it. Maria set it up.

"I've got it!" Kimberly called.

"Mine!" Ellen yelled at the same time.

Elizabeth clenched her fists as she watched both girls step forward. At this point, beating Cedar Springs was going to be tough. If they didn't play together as a team, it would be *impossible*.

But instead of colliding, Kimberly and Ellen both jumped back out of each other's way. The ball landed in the sand between them, but Elizabeth almost felt like cheering. Kimberly and Ellen *were* thinking like a team.

But then the girls on Team Cedar Springs started to giggle.

Mandy gave them a disgusted look. "Nice sportsmanship," she said loudly enough so that their front line could hear.

"Thanks," said a Cedar Springs player with curly red hair. "Nice play."

Team Cedar Springs really cracked up at that one.

"Ignore them!" Kimberly ordered her teammates. "Come on, you guys! Wake up. Let's get aggressive and beat these twits!"

Ellen tossed the ball under the net, and Cedar Springs served. The ball flew over the net. Cammi went for it, but this time Ellen dove in front of her and spiked the ball right over the net and into the sand.

"Ellen!" Cammi yelled.

"Oh, be quiet," Kimberly snapped at her. "At least we've got the ball now! I'll serve!" she said, pushing Mandy out of her way.

Elizabeth felt her stomach knot. "Kimberly, you can't—"

Before Elizabeth could finish, the referee blew her whistle. "Team Sweet Valley, watch your rotation. Another slip and you forfeit the game."

Elizabeth took the ball out of Kimberly's hands. "As I was about to say, you can't serve just because you feel like it. It's my turn."

"Just don't mess it up," Kimberly hissed.

Elizabeth rolled her eyes. *Just when I was thinking*

Kimberly wasn't that bad, she turns back into a snake, she thought as she served the ball.

Elizabeth's serve landed in the net.

"Nice going, Wakefield," Kimberly said as the girls from Cedar Springs slapped high fives.

Ellen rolled her eyes. "If you want something done right, you have to do it yourself."

"No kidding," Kimberly said with a snort.

The red-haired Cedar Springs player stepped into position to serve. She smacked the ball right to Cammi. Cammi was ready for it. But as she jumped to block, Kimberly slammed into her and knocked her to the ground. The ball landed in the sand. Another ace for Cedar Springs.

Elizabeth groaned. *If Kimberly keeps this up, we can kiss this game good-bye.*

"That's the game," the referee said a few minutes later. "Cedar Springs wins 15–4. Next game in fifteen minutes."

"The ref sounds relieved," Maria whispered to Elizabeth.

"She's not the only one," Elizabeth muttered.

Mr. Caldwell looked surprised as the girls surrounded him on the bench. "How did it go?" he asked, without looking up from the papers he was working on.

"If you just bothered to watch, you'd know!" Mandy told him.

Looking embarrassed, Mr. Caldwell set aside the papers he was looking at. "I'm sorry, girls. I know I haven't been much of a coach to you. It's just that I have to get this lineup finished for the swim team's next meet. So, what happened?"

"We lost," Elizabeth said glumly.

"Well, you'll catch up in the next game," Mr. Caldwell said cheerily.

Elizabeth slumped down in the sand. *That will be the day,* she thought. *Winning takes cooperation. And the only time this team cooperates is during drills meant to teach cooperation.* Suddenly, Elizabeth sat up straight. Something had just hit her.

"I know what we have to do!" Elizabeth exclaimed, jumping to her feet. "We have to make a three-hit rule."

Ellen frowned at her. "What are you talking about?"

"We all have to pledge to hit the ball three times," Elizabeth said excitedly. "Even if there's a killer spike opportunity. Even if an opponent's way out of position."

"But that's stupid," Cammi said. "We'll never win like that."

"And we'll never win if Kimberly knocks you unconscious trying to get to the ball," Elizabeth said. "We have to agree to use all three hits. We need the discipline!"

Kimberly rolled her eyes. "Oh, please!"

Ellen made a face and shook her head. "That makes no sense at all."

Elizabeth glanced around at the rest of her teammates. She could tell that some of them knew what she was talking about. Maria looked as if she was carefully considering the possibility.

"We do need to practice our teamwork," Mandy agreed at last.

A smile slowly formed on Cammi's face. "For Sandra," she said, reaching out to shake Elizabeth's hand.

One by one, the other girls put their hands on top of Elizabeth's and Cammi's.

Elizabeth looked at Ellen and Kimberly, who remained outside the circle. "Well? You remember what Sandra said, right? We have to think like a team."

Kimberly folded her arms. "Of course I remember."

Elizabeth sighed. These girls certainly weren't going to make this easy. "Well, the rest of the team is interested in cooperation. What about you guys? For Sandra."

Kimberly's eyes flashed. Then she stepped forward. "Don't get me wrong, Wakefield. I'm not doing this for you." She put her hand firmly on top of the others. "I'm doing it for Sandra."

Elizabeth tried not to grin too broadly. "Ellen?"

"Well." Ellen cleared her throat and stepped forward too. "I guess I'll do it for Sandra also."

Elizabeth felt her heart soar. "All right, then. For Sandra!"

"For Sandra!" everyone chorused.

"One, two, three," Elizabeth counted quietly to herself during the first play in the next game against Cedar.

On the third count, Ellen dinked the ball over the net and scored.

During the next play, Maria counted along with Elizabeth.

By the third play, all of Team Sweet Valley were chanting together. "One! Two! Three!"

The red-haired girl from Cedar Springs nudged one of her teammates. They started whispering to each other furiously. Elizabeth giggled to herself. It seemed as if Cedar Springs thought Team Sweet had some strange new strategy to unnerve them—and in a way, they were right!

During the next play, Elizabeth and her teammates chanted even louder—and they scored again.

"Time out!" called the Cedar Springs captain as soon as the ball hit the sand. Cedar Springs huddled quickly.

"What are they talking about?" Maria asked nervously.

"I don't know," Elizabeth said.

The referee blew her whistle, signaling the end of Cedar Spring's time-out. When the Cedar Springs players stepped back into position, they were all smiling.

That made Elizabeth nervous.

Cammi served.

Cedar Springs returned the ball.

Team Sweet Valley followed their three-hit rule. On *three* Elizabeth hit the ball back. A tall blond girl from Cedar Springs was ready. She whomped the ball right back over the net for the score.

As Elizabeth passed the ball under the net, the blond girl smiled at her. "Are you going to keep this up for the rest of the game?" she asked snidely.

"Stick around and find out," Elizabeth said.

"Oh, I'm not going anywhere," the girl replied. "Although the game did just get less interesting. Now we know exactly what you're going to do on every play."

Elizabeth gritted her teeth. She knew that the three-hit strategy was important for her team, but she had to admit the other girl had a point. Sweet Valley's game had become very predictable.

After the match, Elizabeth pedaled home slowly. Round one was over. Cedar Springs used their advantage to win the second game 15–10. Sweet Valley's record was now two wins, two losses. Competition to get into the play-offs was going to be *very* tight. Depending on how the other teams had done in their matches that day, Sweet Valley could be out of the running. After all they had gone through, when they were finally learning what it meant to be a team, that seemed too cruel. *Please let us make it*, Elizabeth thought.

"I just got off the phone with Kimberly!" Maria breathlessly told Elizabeth on the phone after dinner that evening. "Guess what?"

"Sandra got out of the hospital?" Elizabeth guessed excitedly.

"Well, no," Maria said, sounding a little deflated. "But it's almost as great!"

"Tell me!" Elizabeth exclaimed.

"Mr. Caldwell called Kimberly," Maria said in a rush. "He'd just gotten off the phone with an official from the California Games. We're tied for a position in the play-offs!"

"Tied?" Elizabeth repeated. "What does that mean?"

"It means we play El Carro tomorrow," Maria said.

"El Carro!" Elizabeth yelled. "We already beat them once!"

"I know," Maria said. "And if we do it again, we're in the play-offs!"

Elizabeth's heart seemed to skip a beat. "And if we win in the play-offs—"

"We go to the California Games!" Maria yelled.

"It's really coming down!" Mrs. Slater said the next afternoon. The volleyball team was heading up to El Carro to play their tiebreaker. Mr. Caldwell hadn't been able to get a van on such short notice, so he was driving half of the team in his car. Elizabeth, Cammi, and Maria were getting a ride with Maria's mom.

Elizabeth peered out the car window. Cars were crawling down the beach highway. The rain was falling so hard, it formed a thin sheet of water over the road. The ocean was a steely gray.

"Do you think they'll call off the game?" Maria asked.

Elizabeth shrugged. "I don't know. But you almost sound as if you wish they would!"

"I wouldn't mind actually," Maria admitted. "I'm so nervous, my hands are shaking!"

Cammi turned around in her seat. "I hope we get to play," she said. "I don't think I could stand the suspense much longer."

"Me neither," Elizabeth said breathlessly. In the next hour, Team Sweet Valley just might qualify for the play-offs.

"How can we play in this weather?" Elizabeth yelled to Maria. "The wind will blow the ball all over the place!"

"This wind might blow *us* over!" Maria yelled, wrapping her arms around her chest.

Mrs. Slater had just parked her car in the El Carro beach parking lot. The storm seemed to be getting worse. The wind and rain were so loud, the girls had to shout to be heard.

Mr. Caldwell pulled his car into the spot next to Mrs. Slater's. As Kimberly, Ellen, and Mandy climbed out, the wind drove the rain right into their faces.

Mr. Caldwell, Mrs. Slater, and the girls dashed to the court. A referee wearing a huge orange slicker was waiting for them.

"Is this the Sweet Valley team?" she asked.

"Yes!" Mr. Caldwell yelled.

"Do you have your game form?" the referee asked.

Mr. Caldwell nodded. He pulled some papers out of his jacket and handed them over. "Are we going to play?" he asked.

"We have to," the referee said. "The qualifier is tomorrow, so postponing this match is impossible."

Maria and Elizabeth traded looks.

"We'd better get stretched out," Kimberly said.

The girls spread out across the sand and quickly stretched.

"Maybe we should hit a ball around," Ellen suggested. "We could get some practice with the wind before El Carro shows up."

"Good idea!" Mandy yelled.

Cammi ran to Mr. Caldwell's car and got a ball. Back on the court, she hit the ball over the net. Elizabeth moved to where she thought the ball was going. But a strong wind picked up the ball and carried it toward the foul line. The ball hit the sand. Elizabeth picked it up and discovered it was coated in wet sand.

"This is going to be a strange game!" she called out.

"I wish they'd get here!" Maria exclaimed.

"Tell me about it!" Mandy yelled back.

"I think this is kind of fun!" Cammi said with a laugh. "It reminds me of making mud pies when I was a kid."

Just then a huge bolt of lightning lit up the sky. Then there was a loud crack of thunder.

"Yikes!" Kimberly yelled.

"Let's take a break!" Maria suggested.

The girls ran under the tiny shelter where the referee, Mr. Caldwell, and Mrs. Slater stood chatting.

"Maria, you're all wet!" Mrs. Slater exclaimed.

Maria shrugged. "I'm going to get much wetter once the match begins."

The referee glanced at her watch. "Actually, I'm beginning to doubt there's going to be a match. Our official start time is three o'clock. By league rules, a team forfeits the match if they don't show up within ten minutes of match time. But considering the weather—and the importance of the match—I'm giving El Carro an extra five minutes."

"So how much time do they have left?" Kimberly asked.

"One minute," the referee told her.

The girls all turned toward the parking lot. Elizabeth could feel the blood coursing through her veins. She slowly counted to sixty. No sign of El Carro.

The referee blew a short blast on her whistle. "El Carro officially forfeited this game at three-fifteen. The win goes to Team Sweet Valley."

Elizabeth sucked in her breath. "I can't believe it!"

"We're going to the play-offs!" Kimberly yelled.

Maria grabbed Elizabeth's arm and pulled her out into the rain. The girls started to dance around in circles.

"We're going to the play-offs, we're going to the play-offs!" they chanted. Cammi, Ellen, Kimberly, and Mandy joined them.

Then Elizabeth grabbed Cammi, who grabbed Mandy, who grabbed Ellen and Kimberly. Pretty soon, the girls were all dancing around in circles. "We're going to the play-offs, we're going to the play-offs!" they chanted, and Elizabeth didn't care that she was soaked to the bone.

ELEVEN

"Good luck later, Elizabeth!" Todd Wilkins yelled on Friday afternoon.

Elizabeth looked up from her locker to see her sort-of boyfriend hurrying down the hall. "Thanks!" she called back.

Maria shifted her books to her other arm. "Is Todd coming to the game this afternoon?" she asked.

"Yep," Elizabeth told Maria as she finished choosing her books. "So are all of his friends."

"I guess practically everyone in the sixth grade will be there," Maria said. "Lots of the seventh graders who know Kimberly are going to show up too."

"Jessica told me all of the Unicorns are coming," Elizabeth said as the girls walked out of the school building. "Janet Howell ordered them all to go and support Ellen, Mandy, and Kimberly."

"What, Janet doesn't care about the rest of us?" Maria asked, putting on an offended face.

Elizabeth laughed. "According to Janet, the rest of us are just there to help the Unicorns win!"

Maria bit her lip. "Do you really think we might win? Last time we played Big Mesa, they beat us into the sand!"

Elizabeth took a deep breath. "Well, they're not going to beat us this time."

"How do you know?" Maria asked.

"I don't, really," Elizabeth admitted. "I'm just trying to think positive."

"Think positive," Maria repeated. "I'll try to remember that!"

"There's Jessica," Maria said when she and Elizabeth got to the beach.

Elizabeth scanned the stands, which were crowded with kids and parents. She spotted Jessica sitting with a crowd of Unicorns and waved to her.

Jessica gave her a thumbs-up.

Elizabeth also noticed a big group of kids she didn't recognize. Most of them were wearing black and gold.

"They must be Big Mesa's fans," Elizabeth murmured to Mandy, who was stretching out near their team bench. "I can't believe so many of them came to Sweet Valley for a game."

"Didn't anyone tell you that this is an important match?" Mandy joked. "Whoever wins goes to the California Games."

The California Games, Elizabeth thought. Just

the words made her heat beat faster. She could hardly believe how close Sweet Valley was to making it. And she wasn't planning on letting Big Mesa stop them.

"Team meeting!" Kimberly shouted.

Maria and Elizabeth joined the other girls who were gathering around Kimberly on the sand next to the court.

"OK, guys," Kimberly said once everyone had made a circle around her. "This is it. If we don't win this game, we don't qualify. So, we need to have a vote. Do you want to keep Elizabeth's three-hit rule for this game?"

Elizabeth looked around the circle. She could feel the tension in the air. It was an important decision.

I wish Sandra were here, Elizabeth thought. *She would know what to do.*

Ellen was the first one to speak up. "I think we should drop it," she suggested. "Big Mesa is a great team. If we use the three-hit rule, our game will be totally predictable."

"If we use the rule, Big Mesa will definitely have an advantage," Maria added. "I think we should drop it too. What do you think, Elizabeth?"

Elizabeth bit her lip. A part of her was worried Sweet Valley would stop playing like a team the moment they dropped the strategy. But she knew the other girls were right. They wouldn't have a chance against Big Mesa otherwise. "Drop it," she said at last.

"Yeah, I guess we should," Cammi added

slowly. "But I want you guys to stay off my turf."

"We will," Elizabeth said firmly. "Right, Kimberly?"

Kimberly rolled her eyes. "Sure," she said in a put-upon voice. "So are we in agreement?"

"Yes," Cammi said, somewhat reluctantly.

"Au revoir, rule!" Mandy exclaimed.

"OK, then," Kimberly said tensely. "No three-hit rule. But don't forget that everyone needs to play their best today. Let's concentrate! And let's win!"

Elizabeth looked around at the determined faces of her teammates. *Someone is missing,* she thought. "I wish Sandra were here today," she said, her voice catching.

Maria's eyes were sad. "I'm sure she wishes she were here too."

Ellen shrugged. "Do you actually think she's lying around in her hospital bed thinking about us? She has bigger things to worry about."

"I don't know," Cammi said quietly. "I got the feeling that this team was pretty important to her. She really gave us her all."

"Yeah, and look at how we paid her back," Mandy said, glancing down at her feet.

"What do you mean?" Ellen asked.

Mandy looked up and met Ellen's glare. "I mean, we let her down when she really needed us."

Elizabeth nodded. "Even when she passed out that day, we couldn't . . . you know . . . think like a team."

Kimberly gave Elizabeth a hard look, and Elizabeth stiffened. Was Kimberly going to start leveling accusations at her, blaming her for how things turned out?

But instead Kimberly's face softened. "I keep wishing we'd gotten the ambulance here more quickly," she said quietly. "It might have helped Christopher."

Elizabeth nodded sadly.

For a long moment, nobody spoke. Elizabeth's chest ached. She would have done anything to change what had happened at practice the day Sandra had collapsed. But of course, that was impossible.

The referee blew her whistle. "Let's go!" she called.

Elizabeth looked at her teammates. "Come on, you guys!" she said. "Let's win this for Sandra!"

"For Sandra!" the other girls echoed.

Big Mesa's first serve whizzed over the net.

Elizabeth immediately jumped up to block it. The ball was coming so quickly, she was almost too late. Almost, but not quite. The ball flew toward the back of the court at an awkward angle.

"Mine!" Ellen called. She had to dive into the sand to save the ball. But she managed to get it up high and in front of the net.

"Arrgh," Cammi grunted as she punched the ball over the net.

"Yes!" Kimberly shouted.

The ball was moving toward the sand at a sharp angle. Big Mesa would need a miracle to return it. A girl in Big Mesa's front line dove for the ball and reached it just before it hit the sand. A moment later, the ball was flying right back in Elizabeth's face.

Elizabeth jumped up to block. As she did, she saw an unguarded patch of sand out of the corner of her eye. She pulled her arm back just as she would for a spike. Then she gently tapped the ball over the net, aiming for the unguarded patch. Before Big Mesa could react the ball had hit the sand.

The crowd went crazy. "Wake-field! Wake-field!"

"That was beautiful!" Maria told Elizabeth, her eyes shining.

Kimberly patted Elizabeth on the back. "We're on a roll now!"

Elizabeth let out her breath in a rush. That first play had told her one thing: Beating Big Mesa wasn't going to be easy. They were playing hard. They were just as hungry for a win as Sweet Valley was.

"Wake up out there!" Lila shouted from the bleachers.

"That's all right, Maria!" Jessica shouted. "You'll get it next time!"

Lila slumped back in her seat. "I can't believe Maria missed that ball."

"Oh, give her a break," Jessica said. "Big Mesa hit it awfully hard."

"I bet I could have saved it," Lila said, flipping her hair over her shoulder.

Yeah, right, Jessica thought. Lila was actually an awful volleyball player. She never wanted to dive for balls because she was afraid she'd break a nail.

"Miss, miss, miss," Lila chanted as Big Mesa got ready to serve.

Jessica stared at Lila. "Since when did you get so interested in volleyball?"

"Since Janet ordered us to," Lila replied.

Jessica glanced over her shoulder to the seat where Janet was sitting. Then she smirked. "I don't think Janet is paying too much attention to your cheering."

Lila turned to look too. Janet wasn't paying any attention to the game. She was too busy flirting with a couple of tall guys wearing Big Mesa T-shirts.

"That fink!" Lila exclaimed.

Jessica couldn't help but giggle. Personally, she liked watching Janet fail in her loyalty to the Unicorns sometimes.

Down on the court, Ellen was getting ready to serve. The score was 15–14 in favor of Sweet Valley. If Ellen aced this serve, Sweet Valley would win the first game.

A hush fell over the crowd.

Ellen served. Jessica held her breath as the ball flew over the net. Big Mesa returned it neatly. Cammi jumped up and blocked the ball. Elizabeth set it up for Kimberly, who hammered it over the net.

"Game!" Jessica shouted, jumping to her feet.

But her excitement was premature. A girl on Big Mesa's team punched the ball right back in Kimberly's face.

Jessica slumped back in her seat, deflated. It wasn't fair. She wanted Sweet Valley to win so badly. Why couldn't Big Mesa just give up?

*   *   *

Now! Maria thought at the precise moment Kimberly jumped to block the ball. She relaxed slightly when she saw that Kimberly's hit was textbook perfect. Ellen took a step backward to set up the ball. It soared over Maria's head, in the ideal spot to spike. Maria hammered the ball over the net, feeling more forceful than ever. Big Mesa couldn't get near the ball.

The referee blew her whistle. "The game goes to Sweet Valley!" she hollered.

Maria went weak with relief. One more win and they'd go to the California Games.

"Wasn't that great?" Jessica asked Lila. "I'm so happy we won."

But Lila was gone.

It only took Jessica a second to spot her friend. Lila was a few rows above her in the stands—sitting with Janet and the cute guys from Big Mesa.

Talk about traitors!

Game point, Elizabeth thought with dread toward the end of the second game. Big Mesa was winning 14–12. And they had control of the ball. In order to win, Sweet Valley had to stop their next serve, get the ball down on Big Mesa's side, and win the next four points in a row.

One thing at a time, Elizabeth told herself. She took a deep breath, faced Big Mesa, and got ready for the serve.

"I've got it!" Mandy yelled as the ball soared over the net. She jumped high in the air, but not high enough. Her fingertips barely grazed the ball.

Elizabeth dove for it. But she was too late. The ball rolled into the sand.

The referee's whistle sounded shrilly. "Game Big Mesa!" she called.

Elizabeth sat on the sand and watched the Big Mesa players slap one another on the back. Sweet Valley had lost their lead. The match was tied. Elizabeth had to take a deep breath to keep from crying.

"I can't believe we lost," Kimberly said angrily as she stomped off the court after the second game.

"We played a good game," Cammi told her.

"That's right," Mandy agreed. "We did our best."

Kimberly spun around to face them. She didn't expect any better from Cammi, but hearing this goody-goody routine from Mandy—a Unicorn—infuriated her.

"We did our best," Kimberly said in a mocking voice. "Save it for your mother! We lost. *That's* not our best."

Mandy and Cammi stared at Kimberly.

Then Mandy calmly walked toward the bench. "I don't want to fight with you, Kimberly," she said softly. "Especially not now."

Ellen walked up to Kimberly and offered her a cup of juice. "Hey—mellow out. Here, drink this."

Kimberly took the juice. But she couldn't calm down. *If we don't win the next game, we aren't going to the California Games,* she thought. *One more game and it could all be over.* Kimberly swallowed the juice in one gulp and crushed the empty cup in her hand. *Well, then, we can't lose the next game,* she decided. *We're going to win even if I have to make it happen all by myself. Kimberly Haver is no loser.*

Concentrate! Elizabeth ordered herself.

It was the middle of the third game. Elizabeth was getting ready to serve, but all she could think about was the last play. Kimberly had actually *shoved* Cammi out of the way to get at the ball. Now Cammi looked like she was about to burst into tears. And Kimberly was frowning with such determination it was frightening. *I've got to find a way to hold the team together,* Elizabeth told herself. But she didn't have any brilliant ideas. It was hard to think when hundreds of people were staring at you, waiting for you to start moving.

Elizabeth took a deep breath and closed her eyes. She forced herself to think about nothing but getting the ball over the net. Then she opened her eyes and carefully served. The ball went into the net.

The crowd groaned.

Elizabeth could feel her face burning. How could she have made such a stupid mistake in this incredibly important game?

Ellen picked up the ball and passed it under the net to Big Mesa. Then she turned around and shook her head at Elizabeth.

Elizabeth felt like crawling away and hiding.

"Hey, it happens," Maria said.

Elizabeth nodded. She tried to forget about her mistake. She had Big Mesa's serve to worry about now.

But her concentration was gone. Before she knew what was happening, Team Sweet Valley was trailing 5–9.

We're six points from extinction, Elizabeth thought glumly. *If I'm going to do something, I've got to do it now.* But before Elizabeth could do a thing, Big Mesa served. Cammi and Ellen both jumped to block the ball.

Wham! Cammi and Ellen crashed right into each other. The ball hit the sand.

That made the score 10–5. Big Mesa only needed five more points and they'd be going to the California Games instead of Team Sweet Valley.

A girl from Big Mesa reached under the net and quickly snatched up the ball.

I need time out to think, Elizabeth told herself as she watched the ball being passed back to the server. *I need a time-out!* But only the team captain was allowed to call time-outs.

"Kimberly!" Elizabeth hissed.

"Not now," Kimberly said without turning around. "They're about to serve."

"Kimberly, call a time-out," Elizabeth insisted.

"What's the problem?" Kimberly demanded.

"Just do it," Elizabeth said. "Fast!"

Kimberly groaned loudly. "Time-out!" she called to the referee.

The referee blew a quick blast on her whistle. "You have three minutes," she told the girls.

Kimberly stomped to the sidelines and spun around to face Elizabeth. "What's the big emergency?" she demanded.

"I just thought we could use some time to collect

ourselves," Elizabeth said meekly. "Things aren't going so well out there."

"I noticed!" Kimberly snapped. "So what did you want to say?"

"I-I-I don't know," Elizabeth stammered, feeling flustered.

"Well, I have something to say," Cammi said, stepping closer to Kimberly. "Quit hogging the ball! You stopped me from making two blocks."

"Cammi has a point," Elizabeth said as calmly as she could. "When we work together, we're really a great team."

"Some of us are great," Kimberly retorted. "Some of us haven't even learned how to serve yet."

Elizabeth's patience snapped. How dare Kimberly bring up the one serve she had missed? "Give me a break!" she shouted. "You're the reason we're losing this game! You think—"

"I think what?" Kimberly challenged Elizabeth.

Elizabeth pointed a finger in Kimberly's face. "You think you're better than the rest of us. Well, believe me—"

Mandy gasped. "I don't believe it!"

"Believe me—" Elizabeth repeated, trying to focus on Kimberly.

"No way!" Maria exclaimed, her eyes widening. "Look, Elizabeth."

Elizabeth sighed impatiently. "What is so important?" she demanded as she spun around to look where Maria was pointing. A familiar figure was making her way through the crowd. It was Sandra!

Elizabeth thought she might be imagining things. "Is—is that Sandra?" she asked.

Kimberly started to laugh. "I can't believe it either!" Elizabeth gazed up at the stands. Sandra looked just like her old self. When she noticed the team staring at her, she gave them a thumbs-up. And she was even smiling!

Elizabeth met Kimberly's gaze. Suddenly, telling Kimberly what she thought of her didn't seem so urgent. What was important now was showing Sandra they could pull together and play like a team—just like she had taught them.

"Our time-out is just about over," Kimberly said quietly. "We don't have anymore time to fight. We've got to get serious about winning."

"And that means playing together," Elizabeth added.

Kimberly nodded firmly. "Right."

Sweet Valley got control of the ball on the very next play.

Finally, a chance to catch up, Elizabeth thought.

Elizabeth glanced back from the front row to see whose turn it was to serve. Her heart sank when she saw it was Cammi. If Cammi messed up, the ball would go back to Big Mesa and Sweet Valley might never get another chance to score. Big Mesa only needed five points to win. One bad serve and Cammi could lose them their chance to go to the California Games.

No, that's not fair, Elizabeth told herself firmly. *If we lose, it won't be any one player's fault.*

We've all made plenty of mistakes in this match.

"Go, Cammi!" Elizabeth yelled.

Elizabeth could see how tense Cammi was as she carefully studied the Big Mesa team for a weakness.

Cammi served quickly. The ball made it over the net—but it was heading for the foul line.

Elizabeth held her breath.

None of the Big Mesa players stepped forward. *They think it's going to be out,* Elizabeth realized. The ball hit the sand.

"Was it in?" Cammi called to the referee.

"It was clean," the referee called back.

"Sweet!" Mandy yelled.

Smiling modestly, Cammi stepped back into the service area. Elizabeth passed the ball back to her. Cammi calmly served another ace.

"Yes!" Maria yelled as she and Elizabeth slapped high fives.

Cammi was grinning happily.

"The score is seven to ten," the referee called out.

Elizabeth scanned the stands for Sandra. She didn't spot her. But Elizabeth knew she was there somewhere, cheering them on. That fact made Elizabeth feel terrific.

Cammi served again. This time, the massively tall Big Mesa team captain blocked it. When the ball whizzed over the net, Ellen blocked it neatly. Kimberly hit the ball so it soared up high just in front of the net. Mandy spiked it with all her might.

A Big Mesa player dove for the ball. But all she got was a nose full of sand. The ball hit the sand with a satisfying *thud.*

Elizabeth spun around and gave Cammi a quick hug, then turned to Kimberly. "Great setup!" she told her.

"Thanks," Kimberly said, her eyes shining with excitement.

The ball came back to Cammi. She served.

Two Big Mesa players went for the ball. In their haste, they knocked each other over. They both ended up on their rear.

Maria giggled.

"Hey, don't laugh," Elizabeth teased her. "That must have been how we looked in a lot of our games."

Maria grinned. "Pretty stupid, huh?"

Elizabeth nodded. She was feeling so happy she didn't even mind when Cammi hit her next serve into the net. Nobody else seemed to mind either. Thanks to Cammi, the score was 10–9. Sweet Valley was only one point behind!

"Go! Go! Go!" The Sweet Valley fans were on their feet. They were stomping so hard the bleachers were shaking.

Elizabeth could see Jessica in the middle of the crowd. She was cheering louder than anyone else. All of the time Jessica had put in with the Boosters showed. Her whole row was cheering in perfect unison.

Then Elizabeth heard the sound of a strong, familiar voice on the sidelines. "Go get 'em, girls!"

Elizabeth turned, her eyes wide. Sandra had pulled up a chair to her old spot on the sidelines.

She wasn't prowling around like she would have been before, but she was yelling as loudly as ever.

Maria and Elizabeth exchanged happy looks. Having Sandra there felt so right, Elizabeth's tension about the game started to fade away. It was almost as if the last horrible week had been a bad dream.

Elizabeth turned back to the game. Part of her couldn't wait for the match to end so that she could talk to Sandra. But Elizabeth knew she wouldn't have to wait much longer. For better or worse, the game would be over soon.

While Big Mesa was serving, they'd pushed the score to 13–9. But thanks to another one of Elizabeth's fake-out spikes, Sweet Valley gained possession of the ball.

Kimberly stepped into the service area.

The fans from Big Mesa groaned.

They were right to worry. Elizabeth had never seen Kimberly serve better. Her first serve was a powerful ace that seemed to unnerve Big Mesa. On the next two plays, they missed easy returns. Next was a point-making spike by Cammi. And then another ace. That made the score 14–13. One more point and Sweet Valley would win!

TWELVE

Kimberly thoughtfully tossed the ball from hand to hand as she prepared to serve.

One more point and we're going to the California Games! Elizabeth thought.

The crowd was so quiet, Elizabeth could hear the waves in the ocean breaking.

Kimberly pulled back her arm and hit the ball over the net.

A Big Mesa player jumped to block. With a panic-stricken look, she immediately hit the ball over the net.

That was a mistake, Elizabeth thought. Automatically, she moved into an open position.

Sure enough, Mandy easily blocked the ball.

That's one, Elizabeth thought.

Ellen had plenty of time to step forward and plan her pass. She glanced toward Elizabeth and hit the ball to the exact spot Elizabeth wanted it.

Two, Elizabeth thought.

Elizabeth jumped as high as she could. "Three!" she yelled as she smashed the ball into the sand on the Big Mesa side.

Point, game, and match!

A perfect play, Elizabeth thought happily.

"We won!" Maria screamed, throwing her arms around Elizabeth.

"We're going to the Games!" Ellen shouted as the rest of the team joined the hug.

Elizabeth looked over Maria's shoulder and spotted Sandra. She was standing on the sidelines, beaming at them.

"Sandra!" Elizabeth yelled, breaking free of her teammates and hurrying over to her. Maria followed, and the rest of the team was right behind her.

Elizabeth rushed forward to give Sandra a hug. But at the last second, she hung back. *I don't want to hurt her,* Elizabeth thought. But then Sandra opened her arms. Elizabeth slipped into them and hugged her gently.

"That was a beautiful game!" Sandra exclaimed between hugs with Ellen and Kimberly and Mandy and Cammi and Maria. "I'm so proud of you girls. I can tell how hard you've been working without me!"

"But we only won because of you!" Maria protested. "Seeing you here made us pull our act together."

Sandra laughed and shook her head. "You guys are the ones who deserve the credit."

Having Sandra back was so terrific that Elizabeth

felt like laughing out loud. But she couldn't stop thinking something was different—something about Sandra. Suddenly, it came to her. Sandra's stomach was flat! And that made Elizabeth think of the baby.

Elizabeth's heart started to pound. "How's Christopher?" she asked Sandra quietly, almost afraid to hear the answer.

Tears welled up in Sandra's eyes. And then she broke into an enormous grin. "Christopher is wonderful," she replied. "He's a real trooper. He came home from the hospital this morning."

"That's great," Cammi whispered.

Mandy giggled. "You should have brought him!"

"I thought I'd wait until he's at least a month old before I start dragging him to volleyball games," Sandra said with a wicked smile.

Elizabeth smiled back at her. *Winning is great,* she thought. *But Sandra's good news is even better.*

"Do you need help with the cake and ice cream?" Mandy asked as she bounded into the Wakefields' kitchen on Sunday afternoon. The baby shower the volleyball team had planned for Sandra was in full swing.

Elizabeth licked a stray drop of ice cream off her palm and happily surveyed the plates in front of her. "I think these are all ready. But you could help me carry them out."

"Sure thing," Mandy chirped.

The girls carried the plates out into the living room. The rest of the Wakefield family was at the beach for the day so Elizabeth and her teammates had the house to themselves. Sandra and the entire team were spread out across the living room, chatting like old friends. Elizabeth could hardly believe the team members had been fighting just a few days earlier. In the days since they'd qualified for the California Games, they'd all been working together to plan the belated shower—and they'd been getting along great.

"This plate of cake is especially for you," Elizabeth told Sandra. "I put double the regular amount of ice cream on it."

Sandra winked at Elizabeth. "Thank you! This really makes the party perfect."

Mandy and Elizabeth exchanged happy looks.

"Did you tell Sandra about the paper?" Maria asked Elizabeth. She was sitting in one of the Wakefields' big chairs and cradling Christopher in her lap. Christopher looked adorable in a tiny blue cap and matching snugglie. But so far, he had slept through his entire party.

"Not yet," Elizabeth replied.

"Tell me what about the paper?" Sandra demanded.

"Our faculty adviser wants to do a whole special issue on the volleyball team!" Elizabeth's eyes were sparkling. "We're the first volleyball team from Sweet Valley to make it to the California Games, so we're major news."

Ellen popped a bite of cake into her mouth. "Sounds like a major amount of work too."

Elizabeth shrugged. "Our story is so dramatic, I think the articles will practically write themselves. The only problem is thinking up a really memorable headline."

"How about 'Unicorn Leads Volleyball Team to Victory'?" Kimberly suggested sweetly.

Cammi tossed a throw pillow at her.

"Hey, it was just a suggestion!" Kimberly protested.

"I have one," Mandy said. "How about 'Volleyball Team Almost Kills Worlds' Most Patient Coach'?"

Sandra held up a hand. "You guys didn't have anything to do with that! But I do have a suggestion. How about 'The Rocky Road to Glory'?"

Elizabeth tapped her chin thoughtfully. "Not bad—*and* it features the name of an ice cream flavor," she said with a laugh.

Everyone groaned.

"Why don't you open your presents, Sandra?" Kimberly suggested.

Sandra spooned up the last of her ice cream and put down her plate. "You girls really shouldn't have gotten me anything."

"Don't worry," Cammi said uneasily. "I don't know about the others, but I just got you a *little* present."

"Me too," Maria said quickly. "We wanted to all chip in for something together. But then—well—we sort of weren't speaking to each other, so—"

"Don't apologize!" Sandra said. She reached for the first present.

Everyone watched as she unwrapped a bunny rattle.

"Thank you, Cammi!" Sandra exclaimed. "It's adorable!"

Cammi? Elizabeth thought. *But that's my present!* Before Elizabeth could figure out how to let

Sandra know about her mistake, she had already started to open her next present. It was a rattle just like the one Elizabeth had brought. Or was it? This rattle had a giraffe handle!

"Thanks, Kimberly," Sandra said with a laugh. "I guess Christopher will always have a rattle when he needs one."

Kimberly and Cammi exchanged embarrassed looks.

Elizabeth suddenly realized what had happened. She and Cammi had brought exactly the same thing. And Kimberly had bought *almost* exactly the same thing. Elizabeth's face felt hot. *I've got to sneak my present away from Sandra before she opens it!* she thought.

But it was too late. Sandra reached for Elizabeth's box.

"Oh, no!" Sandra exclaimed after she had finished unwrapping it. "Elizabeth, I can't believe this! You got me same thing!"

"I'm sorry," Elizabeth said miserably. "This is really awful."

"Not at all," Sandra said, her eyes sparkling. "Any truly fashionable baby has *at least* three rattles."

"How about *four?*" Ellen asked sheepishly.

Sandra's eyes widened. "You didn't!"

Ellen nodded and gave an embarrassed laugh. "I got the same thing. Well, mine has a hippo handle."

Sandra shook her head in disbelief. "What are the odds that four out of the six of you would have the exact same idea?"

Mandy cleared her throat. "Five out of six,

actually." She looked at the other girls. "You guys went to Lullaby Land, right?"

Elizabeth nodded. *This is unbelievable!* she thought.

"Did you guys see that velvet bib?" Maria asked. "What kind a baby wears that?"

Elizabeth turned toward her friend. "You didn't go to Lullaby Land too—did you?"

Maria nodded. "Hippo handle."

Sandra laughed.

Elizabeth started to giggle. "It *is* kind of funny when you think about it."

"You can never have enough animal rattles, if you ask me," Kimberly said, covering her smile with her hand.

Sandra grinned at them. "Now this is what I call thinking like a team!"

We hope you enjoyed reading this book. If you would like to receive further information about available titles in the Bantam series, just write to the address below, with your name and address:

KIM PRIOR
Bantam Books
61–63 Uxbridge Road
London W5 5SA

If you live in Australia or New Zealand and would like more information about the series, please write to:

SALLY PORTER
Transworld Publishers (Australia) Pty Ltd
15–25 Helles Avenue
Moorebank
NSW 2170
AUSTRALIA

KIRI MARTIN
Transworld Publishers (NZ) Ltd
3 William Pickering Drive
Albany
Auckland
NEW ZEALAND

All Transworld titles are available by post from:-
Bookservice by Post
PO Box 29
Douglas
Isle of Man
IM99 1BQ

Credit Cards accepted. Please telephone 01624 675137
or fax 01624 670923

Please allow £0.75 per book for post and packing UK.
Overseas customers allow £1.00 per book for
post and packing.